DEC 21	DATE DUE	
JAN 3 1992		
DEC 14 '95		
DEC 18 '97		
DE 16 02		
NO 01 '09		

F
J
Gondosch, Linda
Who's afraid of
Haggerty house?

Who's Afraid of Haggerty House?

Who's Afraid of Haggerty House?

by Linda Gondosch

illustrated by Helen Cogancherry

Lodestar Books · E. P. Dutton · New York

The author and publisher gratefully acknowledge permission
to reprint lines from "A Time To Talk" by Robert Frost
on page 67. From *The Poetry of Robert Frost* edited by
Edward Connery Lathem. Copyright 1916, © 1969 by Holt,
Rinehart and Winston, Inc. Copyright 1944 by Robert Frost.
Reprinted by permission of Henry Holt and Company, Inc.,
and Jonathan Cape Limited, 32 Bedford Square, London
WC1B 3EL, England, on behalf of the Estate of Robert Frost.

Library of Congress Cataloging in Publication Data

Gondosch, Linda.
  Who's afraid of Haggerty house?
  "Lodestar books."

  Summary: Sixth-grader Kelly's attempt to sell
Christmas cards to the lady in the haunted house
begins a mutually enjoyable friendship for them both,
as well as for their families and friends.
  [1. Old age—Fiction. 2. Friendship—Fiction.
3. Christmas—Fiction] I. Cogancherry, Helen, ill.
II. Title.
PZ7.G587Wg 1987 [Fic] 86-24265
ISBN 0-525-67198-6

Published in the United States by E. P. Dutton,
2 Park Avenue, New York, N.Y. 10016,
a subsidiary of NAL Penguin Inc.

Published simultaneously in Canada by
Fitzhenry & Whiteside Limited, Toronto

Editor: Rosemary Brosnan

Printed in the U.S.A.   W   First Edition
10 9 8 7 6 5 4 3 2 1

to my husband, Werner,
who has been so patient and encouraging

Contents

1

How To Make
a Million Bucks Fast

"I'll be rich!" said Kelly McCoy as she tore open the box from the Bismarck Greeting Card Company. "No more worrying about my measly allowance. When I sell these cards, I'll have plenty of money to go Christmas shopping."

"I've got seventy-six cents," said Kelly's little sister.

Kelly laughed. "Listen to this, Samantha. For every box of cards I sell, I get to keep a whole dollar. If I sell a hundred boxes, I make a hundred dollars! I'm talkin' *big* bucks." She spread the boxes of Christmas cards on the family-room floor. "I bet I could sell three hundred boxes, easy."

"Wow!" Samantha scrambled to look at all the cards.

Kelly held up the seller's sheet with columns for names, addresses, amount of boxes sold, and prices. "I'm going to be a saleswoman, a real supersaleswoman. Me and Jennifer—the two supersaleswomen of Hopper Street. I can't wait."

Just then Kelly's nine-year-old brother, Ben, slammed the front door and charged down the hall into the family room. He stumbled over a box of Christmas cards and flew across the floor, sliding into the sofa. "What's all this?" he asked. "Box Mountain?" He dove into the pile of boxes and picked up one of them to look at closely.

"Stop it, Ben!" cried Kelly. She grabbed the box from Ben's hands and scooped up as many boxes as she could. "Do you have to stomp all over my cards like a crazy elephant? I have to sell these."

Ben snatched a Christmas card with a picture of a cardinal perched on a snowy pine bough. He opened it and read:

At Christmas time and throughout the year,
May Peace and Happiness be yours.

He pressed the card to his chest, tilted his blond head upward, and closed his eyes. "Aw, ain't that sweet."

"Give me that!" said Kelly. "I'll *never* get any peace or happiness as long as you're around."

Ben reached for another card. "Put 'em down, Ben. You're getting fingerprints all over them."

"You're really going to sell these?"

"Every one." Kelly stacked the boxes back into the carton. "You wait and see. By this time next week, I'll be a millionaire. I might even buy you a Christmas present."

Ben flipped open the prize catalog and looked at pages of radios, fishing poles, basketballs, tents, and telescopes.

"What I'd really like is a telescope." He pointed to a picture.

"I want this wagon," said Samantha. She leaned over Ben's shoulder. "Get me this wagon, OK? Please?"

"We'll see," said Kelly. "It all depends on how many cards I sell."

"I sure hope you sell a lot," said Ben.

"I do, too." Kelly slipped into her purple jacket and carried the carton into the front hall. "Maybe I'll just go for the big cash prize. Then I could go shopping at Lorey's. That'd be fun." She opened the front door. A sharp gust of December wind struck her face.

"Hi, Kelly!" Up the McCoys' sidewalk came Kelly's two best friends, Jennifer Jackson and Adelaide Borseman. They pulled a sled that held a large cardboard box with the words *Bismarck Greeting Card Company* on the side.

"Good! I see you got your cards, too," said Kelly. "Ready to make some big bucks? Why don't you take this side of the street, and I'll start over there? Adelaide, d'you want to come with me?"

"I'm done!" said Jennifer. She picked up her empty carton and flipped it upside down. "See? Sold every single box."

"What?"

"It was easy, wasn't it, Adelaide?" Jennifer and Adelaide shook hands like proud business partners. "We had a blast! Yesterday and today, we went up and down Hopper and then over on McConnell and Stewart and Dillard. We must have walked a thousand miles, didn't we, Adelaide?" Jennifer tossed her blonde curls and waved her arms in the air as she spoke. She always exaggerated everything. She was practicing to be a great movie actress.

"Two thousand miles," said Adelaide. Perhaps because she was the tallest girl in the sixth grade, Adelaide tended to hunch forward, as if trying to hide her height. Now she stood in the cold, her arms wrapped around her shoulders. Her teeth chattered. "L-let's go inside. My glasses are beginning to f-freeze to my nose, and my f-fingers are turning into crooked little icicles. Look!" She held up her red hand.

"You should've worn gloves," said Jennifer.

"I can't remember everything," said Adelaide.

"For a person who gets all A's, you'd think you'd re-member your gloves," replied Jennifer. She punched Ade-laide playfully on her shoulder.

"Geniuses don't think about things like g-gloves." She laughed. "Come on, let's go in." She stomped her boots in the snow and thrust her red hands deep into her jacket pockets.

"You mean you're all done?" cried Kelly. She dropped her heavy carton onto the porch floor. "We waited weeks to get these cards, and then I'm gone two days to visit my grandparents, and you run off and sell all your cards without me. Thanks a lot!"

Jennifer looked shocked. "Gosh, Kelly, what's your problem? We never said we had to sell them together, did we?"

"I sure don't want to go around door-to-door all by myself. That's no fun. Why didn't you wait for me?"

"Everyone was out selling cards yesterday," said Jen-nifer. "I had to get started before all the customers were taken."

"Terrific. Well, I'm going now. Are you coming with me?"

4

"Oh, Kelly, I'm sick of selling," said Jennifer. "I hope I never see another doorbell. Anyway, my toes feel like ice cubes."

"Come on," begged Kelly. "I'd go with you."

"Let's go, p-please!" said Adelaide to Jennifer. "I'm half-frozen."

"How about my house for some hot cocoa?" Jennifer asked Adelaide. "Maybe we could make some Rice Krispies treats. Wanna?"

"Yeah!"

Kelly looked at the houses on Hopper Street. "You probably took every customer on the street and all the other streets, too. Anything left for me?"

Jennifer and Adelaide turned to go. "There's still Malvina Krebs," called Jennifer. She leaned toward Adelaide and whispered something in her ear.

"She never buys anything!" Kelly felt her face growing red with anger. She wanted to kick the Bismarck Greeting Card Company box to smithereens. But instead she ran down the porch steps and stuck her foot in front of Jennifer's sled.

"Can't *you* even come with me?" She looked pleadingly at Adelaide.

Adelaide groaned. "Please! I went around yesterday and today. I am *not* going around anymore. This salesman stuff is for the birds."

"Gee, thanks. What'd you go with Jennifer for? Why didn't you wait for me?"

"You're not my boss. I'll go with whoever I want to." Adelaide pushed her glasses higher on her nose and stood up straight. "Anyway, Jen's giving me fifty cents for every box we sold."

"I would have given you fifty cents!"

5

"We're *sorry,* all right?" said Jennifer.

"Get your big foot out of the way," said Adelaide. "Come on, Jennifer. Let's go."

Kelly grabbed Jennifer's empty Bismarck Greeting Card Company box and dumped it upside down on Adelaide's head. Adelaide's glasses slid off her nose and fell into the snow.

"Hey! What'd you do that for?" cried Jennifer.

"My glasses!" yelled Adelaide. She pushed the box from her head and squinted in the sunlight.

"Here they are." Jennifer lifted the glasses from the snow.

"Oh, wonderful! Now they're really frozen." Adelaide glared at Kelly. "What's the matter with you? You could have broken these." Kelly stood there, not knowing exactly what to say. She wanted to say she was sorry, but she didn't *feel* sorry, so she slowly backed up, turned around, and climbed the porch stairs.

"Come on, Jennifer," said Adelaide. "Let's go to your house." She gave Kelly an icy stare.

"Yeah," said Jennifer. "Let's go."

"Go on. Leave," said Kelly. "I'll sell my cards by myself. I'll sell twice as many as you." She picked up the heavy carton. Jennifer and Adelaide walked down the sidewalk, pulling the sled over the snow with the Bismarck Greeting Card Company box bumping along on top.

When she reached the street, Jennifer turned around. "And don't say we didn't leave you any customers. We didn't sell any to that old lady on Stewart Street, either."

"Mrs. Hag, the Old Bag," said Adelaide. She laughed her loud, horsey laugh, complete with three snorts.

"Super," said Kelly. "The Haggerty house is haunted. You didn't go there, did you?"

"Are you kidding?" answered Jennifer. "I wouldn't go there if you paid me one hundred thousand dollars. Malvina Krebs said she saw a ghost standing by the attic window!"

Some friends, thought Kelly. They leave me the haunted Haggerty house over on Stewart Street.

The only reason Kelly even knew old Mr. and Mrs. Haggerty was because all the trick-or-treaters dared each other to climb the long, crumbling stairway to their front door, where they were rewarded with candied apples and shiny new nickels. But the rest of the year, they ran past the house as fast as they could. It had a spooky look about it, on Halloween and every other day.

Kelly sat down on the bottom porch step and propped her chin in her upturned palms. She tried to think where she could sell her Christmas cards. She tried not to think about Jennifer and Adelaide. But try as she might, she could not stop thinking about her two best friends sitting around Jennifer's kitchen table, drinking hot cocoa and having a good time, all without her.

Wham! A snowball hit her right shoulder.

2

The Business Deal

"Gotcha that time!" Ben grinned and scooped up another handful of snow.

"Stop it, Ben! That hurt. Why don't you go and—" Kelly stopped. Ben zapped another snowball straight at the Bismarck Greeting Card Company box. *Whap!* It exploded right on target.

"Hey, maybe *you* could come with me!" Even Ben was better than nobody. Maybe she could figure a way for Ben to do the talking at the door while she waited on the sidewalk.

"Where?"

"To that old Haggerty house over on Stewart Street. I'll give you half the money. Who knows? They might buy ten boxes."

"Mrs. Krebs said the Haggerty house is haunted!" said Ben.

"She said she saw a cross-eyed crocodile, too." Kelly laughed. "You can't believe everything Mrs. Krebs says, Ben."

"Well, that's what she said. Haunted!"

Kelly began to chew her thumbnail, which was what she always did whenever she was nervous. "Never mind. I'll go by myself. I'm not chicken." She started toward the garage to get her sled.

"Are you calling me chicken?" asked Ben. He scooped up a handful of snow.

"I sure am. 'Cause that's what you are. Chicken, chicken! Scaredy-cat! Scared of the monster under your bed. You're scared of everything!"

"The Haggerty house *is* haunted," insisted Ben.

Kelly laughed. "It is not."

"It is, too." Ben rushed up to Kelly, yanked back her jacket, and crammed a snowball down her back.

"Aaaeee!" Kelly howled at the top of her voice as the snow slid down her spine. She hopped up and down like a crazy kangaroo, shaking the snow from her clothes.

"Don't ever call me chicken!" Ben yelled, wagging his finger at her.

"Ooooh, you're really going to get it now, Ben. You're dead!" Kelly ran toward him.

Ben spun around and scrambled up the maple tree. He crawled onto the lowest branch and shook it, dumping a pile of snow directly onto her head. "Bull's-eye!" he shouted. And then he slipped and fell to the ground, squashing her beneath him.

"Get off me, you gorilla!" she screamed.

"Where are you?" asked Ben. He sat on her back, pretending to be in a daze.

"Get off!" Kelly kicked and punched and twisted until suddenly Ben plunged sideways into the snow with a horrible look on his face.

"Ooow!" he cried. "My leg! I think it's broken!" He writhed from side to side, holding his left leg.

"Oh my gosh, Ben!" cried Kelly. She jumped up. "Let me look. No, wait! Don't move. Don't try to stand up. You might make it worse!"

Ben rocked back and forth, grasping his leg just above his boot. "Do something!" he cried. "Get Mom! Please!"

Kelly's face was white. "Don't move. I'll be right back!"

"Hurry!"

"I'm going!" Kelly scrambled across the yard, tripped, picked herself back up, and ran again.

"Is that as fast as you can go?" called Ben. "You look like a five-hundred-pound penguin. If only you could run like me." He sprang to his feet and took off, galloping around the house.

Kelly raced after him, grabbed his arm, and swung him to the ground, smearing his face into the snow.

"Hey!" cried Ben as he spluttered for breath. "Can't you take a joke?" He started to laugh, and soon Kelly was laughing along with him.

"Broken leg, huh?" she said. She straddled his back and held tight to his shoulders, as though riding a rambunctious horse.

"Get off, you five-hundred-pound penguin. Get off and I'll . . . I'll go with you to the spook house."

"You will?"

"I will. I will. I promise!"

"I bet. Cross your heart and hope to die!" ordered Kelly.

11

"OK. OK. Cross my heart and hope to . . . no, I don't ever want to die." He twisted away from Kelly, lay flat on his back in the snow, and crossed his heart. "I probably *will,* though, going to a place like the old spook house. I get half the money, right?"

"You got it." They shook hands.

Kelly looked at her younger brother. He wasn't so bad, after all. She pulled her sled from the garage, put the cardboard box on top, and hurried after him. They cut through Buster Gorden's backyard, crossed the frozen creek, and came out on Stewart Street. As they approached the old Haggerty place, they slowed down. A long flight of broken stone steps led from the front sidewalk to the porch. The house was an old Victorian mansion with a tower on the left corner and dead vines clinging to its walls. Long, dark windows were bordered with green shutters, one of which hung cockeyed. Icicles dripped from the eaves. In the yard, tufts of weeds and long grass stuck up through the melting snow. The fence around it had several broken pickets, and the house itself needed a fresh coat of paint.

"Now there's a job for me," said Ben. "I could cut this grass and fix up the fence and all those shutters next summer."

They stood at the bottom of the steps and gazed at the dilapidated house. "Did you trick-or-treat here on Halloween?" Kelly asked.

"Yeah. We got candied apples and nickels. You should have come. I dared Ernie to go up to the porch, but he wouldn't go. You know Ernie."

"I know."

"He said he didn't want any candied apples *or* pickles,

12

and I told him they gave nickels, not pickles, but he still wouldn't go."

"It's not that bad once you're up there. I think the old lady is nice," said Kelly.

"Mr. Haggerty is weird—never says too much. Just smokes his cigars," said Ben. "I didn't even see him this time. Probably hiding."

"Oh, I don't know. I remember one Halloween he told us a story about a chicken that lived on his farm when he was a little boy. It was the time we went out too early, and Mrs. Haggerty hadn't finished making the candied apples. Don't you remember?"

"Sort of."

"Do you really think this house is haunted?" asked Kelly.

"Are you kidding? Anyone can tell by looking at the place! Malvina Krebs said she was out walking one night and heard some strange noises. She said she saw a misty white thing float straight out that tower window and through the trees." Ben pointed to the dark tower. "Wild, huh?"

"I don't believe it."

"That's what she said," insisted Ben.

"This place is giving me the creeps!"

"Shhh! Look!"

Kelly gripped the sled rope as the front door opened.

3

Hot Chocolate
and Garbage Collectors

Mrs. Haggerty stepped onto the porch. She raised her hand to block the sun and peered down the street, as though she were expecting someone. She waved to Kelly and Ben. They looked at each other and then waved back.

"Oh, come on," said Kelly. "Let's try it. I bet they'll buy ten boxes. Old geezers like them have oodles of money *and* oodles of friends with money." She and Ben climbed the steps, lugging the cardboard box between them.

"Now let me think," Mrs. Haggerty said slowly, studying first Ben and then Kelly. Because of her thick eyeglasses, her eyes seemed twice as big as they really were. She tried to remember back to Halloween. "You must have been the pirate," she said to Ben, "and weren't you a clown?"

"Don't you remember me?" said Ben. "I was a warlock."

"I didn't go trick-or-treating this year. I was too busy with my witch meeting. I'm Kelly McCoy, and this is my brother, Ben. We live over on the next street."

"McCoy. McCoy. McCoy. Of course! Isn't your father Dr. McCoy, that young dentist?"

"Yeah, that's him."

"Doggone it, I wish I'd gone to him instead of that no-account quack I went to. Dr. Snodkins put these awful teeth in." Mrs. Haggerty flipped her upper dentures out with her tongue and then pulled them back in. Kelly and Ben jumped back.

"Listen here. Won't you come in for a bit?" Mrs. Haggerty turned and walked inside, motioning them to follow. "Come on, get along inside now. It's cold out here!"

"How would you two young'uns like some g-o-o-o-d hot chocolate? Hmmm? You look about chilled to the bone." She scurried into the kitchen while Ben plopped down onto a soft chair covered with a well-worn flowered slipcover.

"Don't sit down, Ben," whispered Kelly. "We're not staying that long." She glanced anxiously about the parlor. A goldfish swam in a bowl on top of a walnut table. A TV in the corner was turned on to a soap opera. A picture of Mr. and Mrs. Haggerty and a handsome young man stood on the TV.

"Here we go," said Mrs. Haggerty as she returned with three mugs of hot chocolate. "I put in two big marshmallows. I hope you like marshmallows."

"I love 'em!" said Ben. He pulled off his hat.

"Take off your jackets. Stay awhile." Mrs. Haggerty sat down by the fireplace and folded her hands in her lap. Her face wrinkled with pleasure.

"We were wondering if you'd like to buy some Christmas cards," explained Kelly as she opened the cardboard box and pulled out her samples.

"Christmas cards, did you say?" Mrs. Haggerty stretched her thin arm toward Kelly and took a card. "Ooooh!" It almost seemed as if she had never seen a Christmas card before. She studied the card, fascinated, and then reached for another. "Why, these are very pretty."

"These big ones only cost four ninety-five," said Kelly.

Mrs. Haggerty peered out the low front window. "They're here!"

"Who?" said Ben.

"Joseph and Neely." She laid the cards on the table, stood up, and walked to the front door. Ben and Kelly followed closely behind her. A garbage truck came to a screeching stop in front of the house.

Mrs. Haggerty cupped her hands around her mouth and hollered to the two men on the truck. "I've got some good hot chocolate for you today. Now don't you pass by without stopping in for a bit. Hurry up, now!"

Kelly and Ben backed into the house as the two garbage collectors bounded quickly up the steps and stomped into the front hall. Mrs. Haggerty disappeared into the kitchen.

"Does she always give you hot chocolate?" asked Ben, eyeing the two men.

"Not always," said Neely with a chuckle.

"We get Cokes in the summer," said Joseph.

Back through the kitchen doorway came Mrs. Haggerty, carrying a tray with two mugs. "Sit down, Neely. Here, Joseph. Don't tell me you can't sit a spell on such a blustery day!"

"Oh, we can't stay too long," said Joseph. He blew across the chocolate bubbles.

"We have a few minutes, though," added Neely.

"I want you to see who came to visit me today," said Mrs. Haggerty. "This here's Kelly McCoy and her brother, Ben. They've brought me some mighty pretty cards to look at." Neely and Joseph nodded at Kelly and Ben.

Mrs. Haggerty picked up a sample card with a picture of a church nestled in a snow-covered valley. "Ain't this a sight? Prettiest card I've ever laid eyes on. What do you think?" She poked the card in front of Neely's nose.

"That's real nice," agreed Neely. He sipped his hot chocolate. "Selling cards, kids?"

"We're trying to earn some money to go Christmas shopping," said Kelly.

"How much are they?"

"Three ninety-five for the little ones, four ninety-five for the big ones."

"We make a whole dollar on every box," said Ben. "We're splittin' it. Kelly says we'll be millionaires in a week. I'm gettin' a telescope—"

"Ben!" Kelly glowered at him, and he sat back down on the slipcovered chair.

Joseph whistled. "I don't send many Christmas cards myself." He set his mug on the tray.

"You boys look tuckered out," said Mrs. Haggerty. "Can't you stay awhile?"

"No, no, we've got to be running along," said Joseph. "Work to do."

"Thanks for the hot chocolate," said Neely as he opened the front door.

"There's no sense in you rushing off like this. You come and go like a couple of jackrabbits. I wish you'd stay and warm yourselves by the fire."

"No, ma'am. We'd sure like to, but we'd better be going." Neely and Joseph hopped down the steps two at a time. "See you next week."

"You'll catch your deaths with those flimsy jackets. You ought to bundle up more!" Mrs. Haggerty closed the door behind them and hurried back to the parlor. She smoothed her white hair back and tried to tuck it under some hairpins on the back of her head.

"Those boys don't have a lick of sense," she muttered as she sat down with a grunt. She reached for another sample card.

"I wish you'd look at this little snowman." She held up the card for Kelly and Ben to see.

Kelly listened to the ticking of the grandfather clock that loomed near the doorway. She could hear it over the noise coming from the TV. If Mrs. Haggerty decided to inspect every card, they would be there all day. Kelly studied the ceiling and noticed long, loopy cobwebs hanging from the light fixture.

"I believe I'll take this one here." Mrs. Haggerty pointed to the card with the church in the valley. "That's a fine-looking church. Reminds me of the church I went to when I was a girl. It was down the road a ways from our farm. Papa used to drive us every Sunday morning in a beautiful black buggy. Lordy! I wish you could have seen it."

Kelly pulled out the seller's sheet and filled in Mrs. Haggerty's name and amount paid. Then she handed her a box of cards. "That'll be four ninety-five."

19

Mrs. Haggerty stood up and looked around uncertainly. "Now where is my purse?" She poked about the room, looking under pillows and behind chairs. "Horsefeathers!"

"What's the matter?" asked Kelly.

"My purse is hiding again. I declare, I never can find that purse."

"Oh, that's OK," said Kelly. "We'll stop by tomorrow. Come on, Ben, we'd better get going."

"You have to go? So soon? You haven't even said hi to Clark."

"Clark?"

"My goldfish." Mrs. Haggerty walked to the table where the fishbowl stood. "I named him after a famous movie star. Don't you think he's a handsome little fish?"

"He's not bad for a fish," said Ben. He stared at the fish, his nose pressed flat against the fishbowl.

"Say, Mrs. Haggerty," said Kelly as an idea popped into her head. "You wouldn't happen to have some friends who might need Christmas cards, would you?"

"Friends?" Mrs. Haggerty sprinkled fish food into the bowl. "I've got hundreds of friends. I'll have to get my list. I keep all their names and telephone numbers on a list. Just a minute." She walked into the dining room and then into the kitchen.

Kelly and Ben huddled around the walnut table and tapped on the fishbowl. Suddenly the closet door slammed. Kelly jumped. "What was that?"

"A ghost," said Ben. He pointed to the closet next to the grandfather clock.

"No, really."

"How should I know? It just slammed. *Bam!*" Ben tiptoed toward the closet. Kelly crept behind him.

"Open it," she whispered. "Go on."

"*You* open it."

"No, *you* open it."

"I don't want to," answered Ben.

"You're the biggest chicken in the world," said Kelly as she reached for the doorknob.

"I can't find that list," said Mrs. Haggerty, returning to the parlor. "I can't remember where anything is these days. That's what happens when you get old and scatterbrained like me."

Kelly and Ben spun around. "The list? Oh, don't worry about it." Kelly glanced at the tall rocking chair near the TV. It was the chair Mr. Haggerty always sat in. "How about Mr. Haggerty? Do you suppose he'd like to take a look at our cards?"

"Oh, I know he would, but he isn't here."

"He's not?"

"No, no. You see, he's been ailing a lot lately. He's in the hospital in Louisville."

"Oh, gosh," said Kelly. "That's too bad."

"Gets awful lonesome around here without him, let me tell you."

"I hope he's better real soon. Come on, Ben. We'll never finish selling these cards if we don't get going." Kelly carefully placed all the boxes, the sample cards, and the seller's sheet back inside the Bismarck Greeting Card carton.

Ben followed her to the doorway, pausing as he walked past the closed closet. "This door slammed shut a few minutes ago," he said. "Does it always do that?"

"Slammed shut?" repeated Mrs. Haggerty. "That must have been when I opened the back door into the pantry. There's an awful draft in this house."

Kelly laughed. "Ben thought it was a ghost."

21

"I did not!" said Ben.

"You did, too."

"Well, so did you." Ben pulled on his hat.

"You don't have to rush off like this," said Mrs. Haggerty. "You just got here. Can't you stay a bit? My program is about to come on the television. Don't you want to watch it with me?"

"We can't," said Kelly.

"Well, now, I'll look for that list. Lord knows, I've got hundreds of friends. Can't keep track of 'em all, if you want the truth." She waved as Kelly and Ben carried the Bismarck Greeting Card box down the steps.

"What a weird customer," said Ben.

"She bought a box, didn't she?"

"Do I get a dollar?" asked Ben.

"Fifty cents, as soon as she pays us."

"Don't forget!" Ben took off running, pulling the sled behind him.

"Wait up," called Kelly. They cut through a yard, crossed the frozen creek, and came out on Hopper Street.

Marigold Krebs and Samantha were playing on the sidewalk as Ben came running with the sled. "Look out!" he called. The girls screamed as he swerved around them. The sled veered to the left, hit a bump, and the Bismarck Greeting Card carton sailed through the air. Boxes of cards tumbled from the overturned carton into the snow.

"Ben!" screamed Kelly. "Look what you did!"

"I didn't do anything. Samantha got in my way. Oh, boy, Sam, you're in big trouble!" Ben yelled as he zipped across the street.

"I am not," said Samantha. "I didn't spill 'em. *You* spilled 'em."

"Ben!" yelled Kelly. "Come back here and help me pick this up." Kelly wiped the boxes on her jacket sleeve and pushed them back into the box.

"Guess who called you," said Samantha.

"Who?" Kelly asked.

"Guess." Samantha loved secrets.

Kelly thought of Jennifer and Adelaide. Maybe they had called to beg her forgiveness. Maybe they had finally realized just how mean they had been. Or maybe it was Alex Bradford—the cutest boy in the entire sixth grade. "Who called, Samantha?"

"Will you get me that wagon if I tell?"

"Samantha! Who called?"

"I'm not telling."

4

Dungeons and Spiders

Kelly dialed Adelaide's number.

"Hello?" It was Adelaide. She had a loud voice that was easy to recognize.

Kelly pinched her nose and said with a whine, "This is your operator. Did you recently place a call to 555-2255?"

"That's you, isn't it, Kelly?"

"This is your operator speaking."

"Sure, sure," said Adelaide. "What do you want?"

Kelly gave up. "Did you call before?"

"No."

"Oh. I thought maybe that was you who called."

"Why would I call you, after you almost killed me with that dumb box and practically destroyed my expensive glasses? And I don't appreciate being called Horseface!"

"I never called you Horseface!"

"Yes, you did. Susan told me you called me Horseface in school Friday, behind my back."

"Adelaide, I never called you Horseface! It was Todd who called you Horseface."

"I bet. You always did think I looked like a horse. Isn't that right, Smelly Kelly?"

"Don't call me Smelly Kelly. I hate that."

"Smelly Kelly. Smelly Kelly."

"HORSEFACE!"

"Smelly Kel—"

Kelly slammed down the receiver. She couldn't believe it. One of her very best friends acting like an idiot! Why couldn't they have waited two days so they could all sell their cards together? It just wasn't fair.

Kelly remembered the day in October when she and Jennifer, her best friend ever since kindergarten, had invited Adelaide to join their secret witch coven. Adelaide, the girl who never got invited to join anything. The three of them had become the witches of Hopper Street—Madame Venezuela, Lady LaChoy, and Gypsy Jezabubble. And now it was Jennifer and Adelaide. Jennifer and Adelaide. Kelly was kicked out into the snow like a cockroach-infested log.

She quickly wiped a tear from her cheek as her bedroom door opened and Samantha walked in. Samantha jumped onto the bed.

"What do you want?" asked Kelly.

"Wanna know who called you?" asked Samantha. She bounced up and down on the bed.

"Who?"

"It was Jennifer," said Samantha.

"Are you sure? Did she say she'd call back?"

"Nope. She just wanted to know if you'd sold any Christmas cards yet."

"Is that all?" said Kelly.

"Yep. That's all." Samantha bounced off the bed and ran out of the room.

The next morning, Kelly walked into her Sunday school class with the feeling that her stomach was tied into hundreds of knots. She sat at the far end of the table and didn't answer any of Mrs. Thomas's questions. Jennifer and Adelaide laughed and talked and raised their hands to answer almost all the questions. Kelly pretended to be fascinated by a chickadee that fluttered among the branches of the pine tree outside.

On the way out of class, Jennifer stopped Kelly at the door. "Sell any cards yet?"

"Sure, at least thirty," answered Kelly. "And Mrs. Haggerty's giving me a list of all her friends to sell to, too."

"Old Hag the Bag? No joke!" said Jennifer.

"Come on, Jen," said Adelaide. "Let's sit in the back."

They were gone. Instead of sitting with her two friends in church as she always did, Kelly sat down between her mom and Samantha on one side and her dad and Ben on the other. All through the service, she felt Jennifer's and Adelaide's eyes boring holes through the back of her head. Once she glanced back and saw them whispering together while they read their church magazine.

"Quit kicking me, Samantha," Kelly whispered. "You'll get a run in my new nylons."

"I'm just swinging my legs. My foot fell asleep." Samantha squirmed in the seat beside her.

During the offertory, Kelly noticed a black spider with long, trembling legs crawling across the pew between her and Ben. Ben saw it, too. He reached down, grabbed one

26

of the quivering legs, and then, crossing his arms on his chest, he leaned slowly to the left until the spider tickled Kelly's arm.

"Ben!" Kelly jumped to the left and knocked into Samantha who bumped into Mrs. McCoy. Kelly's mother gave Kelly a cold stare that said *Settle down or else!*

How could she settle down with a spider tickling her arm? She jumped up and squeezed past Samantha and her mother and sat back down at the end of the pew. Ben tossed the spider on the floor and crunched it under his shoe.

That afternoon Kelly had to stay in her room for one hour for being disruptive in church. "But, Dad, Ben was trying to kill me with a hairy tarantula. It was poisonous!"

"I never saw any tarantula," said her father. "Ben says you were pestering him. You know what I told you about talking in church."

"You don't believe *Ben,* do you?"

"Why shouldn't I?"

"Oh, Dad, you always believe Ben. You never believe me."

"That's not true."

"I'm telling you," said Kelly, "he was trying to tickle me with a tarantula."

Dr. McCoy looked at his watch. "You can come out at three o'clock. I want you to sit here and think about what you did."

Kelly sat in her basement bedroom and thought, but not about what she had done. Mainly, she thought about what she was going to do if she ever got her hands on that bratty brother of hers. He got away with everything!

The phone rang once. Kelly grabbed it. It was probably

Adelaide wanting to apologize for calling her Smelly Kelly.

"Oh, Kelly, I'm so glad you're there," said Mrs. Haggerty.

"I'm here, all right." Kelly lay on the floor with her legs on her bed and stared at the ceiling of her jail cell.

"I've found the prettiest cards from all over. I have them here in a shoe box. I have some Christmas cards, some birthday cards, some get-well cards from that time I was in the hospital with my shoulder out of whack." She paused. "Or maybe it was the time my left leg swelled up like a balloon. That laid me up for several weeks. Did I ever tell you about that?"

Kelly shifted the receiver to her other ear. "No, I don't think so. Did you ever find that list of names? You know, all your friends that might need Christmas cards?"

"Fiddle-faddle, I forgot about that list. I got so interested in this box of cards. Come on over. I want you to see these."

I want to sell cards, thought Kelly, not look at them. But she answered, "I'll be over around three, OK?"

"Three o'clock? Good gracious, why not now?"

"'Cause I'm in jail right now."

"You are?"

"My father threw me into the dungeon and bolted the door. I'm a prisoner."

"Mercy!"

"He won't let me have lunch or anything. I'm lucky to still have my telephone. The line might be cut any minute, though."

"Your father? That nice young dentist?"

"Oh, he's nice to his patients, but he hates me. He's

always sending me to my room without any dinner. It isn't easy living here, Mrs. Haggerty. I'm starving!"

"You poor child. You skedaddle over here when you can, and I'll fix you a delicious onion and garlic sandwich. That'll make you feel better. Makes me feel better every time."

"I'll be over in a little while."

Later that afternoon, Kelly climbed the steps to the old Haggerty house and knocked on the door. "You poor young'un," said Mrs. Haggerty. She scrutinized Kelly from head to foot through her thick eyeglasses. "Are you all right?"

"I'm feeling much better now."

"Go fix yourself something. How about one of my onion and garlic sandwiches? They're the tastiest things you ever sunk a tooth into." Mrs. Haggerty practically pushed Kelly to the refrigerator.

"You know what always makes me feel better?"

"What's that?"

"Ice cream."

"Well, for heaven's sake, child, why didn't you say so? I've got ice cream." Mrs. Haggerty opened the freezer door and pulled out a box of vanilla ice cream. "Here. Help yourself."

"Thanks!"

"And put a little chocolate syrup on it. And how about a slice of banana? You're nothing but skin and bones."

"That's because Ben eats all the ice cream at our house," said Kelly. "By the time I get to the freezer, the ice cream's gone. He leaves the empty box for me." She dug into the delicious concoction while Mrs. Haggerty spread a few cards on the table. Kelly studied the postmarks on the yellowed envelopes. San Francisco, 1935; Honolulu, 1941; Pittsburgh, 1956.

"Look at this!" Mrs. Haggerty handed Kelly a small birthday card with a picture of a simple basket of roses. Kelly opened it and read:

This special birthday wish I send—
My love for you will never end.
                                    Arthur

"Arthur gave me this on my last birthday."

"And who's this one from?" Kelly held out a Christmas card with a picture of an old-fashioned family singing carols around a piano. She opened it and read the words scribbled across the bottom: "*I'll be home for Christmas. Tyler.* Who's Tyler?"

"My son," said Mrs. Haggerty. "Oh, he's a fine boy, my Tyler. Here's a picture of him." She pointed to a gold-framed picture on the wall. "Isn't he good-lookin'?"

"Yes, he is. Where does he live?" Kelly checked the postmark.

"Los Angeles."

"Is he coming for Christmas?"

Mrs. Haggerty chuckled. "You don't know my Tyler. He couldn't possibly come, not this year anyway. He's a very busy man, a very important man."

"Really? What does he do?" asked Kelly. She licked the chocolate syrup from her spoon.

"He's a producer, a film producer, busy all the time. I believe he told me he was working on a film about ancient mummies in Peru or somewhere."

"Wow! Ancient mummies. I'd like to see that film. Too bad he's not coming for Christmas, though."

"Yes, it is too bad. Maybe next year." Kelly followed Mrs. Haggerty into the library. Shelves and shelves of dusty books lined the walls from floor to ceiling. A tall upright piano stood in the corner by a window.

"Have a seat. I want to show you my book." Mrs. Haggerty handed her a book of poems. "Isn't this beautiful? Tyler sent me this last Christmas. He knows how fond I am of Robert Frost's poems."

"Read me one," coaxed Kelly, handing the book back. Mrs. Haggerty took the book and looked closely at page 1. "I'd like to, sure enough. Maybe later. My eyes are hurting me some today." She closed the book and laid it gently on a table. "Well now, if I don't give you that four ninety-five, I'll forget where I put it."

"Yeah, I guess I better be going."

"You don't need to go yet. You haven't even heard my song!" Mrs. Haggerty hurried over to the piano and shuffled through some papers in the piano bench.

"What song?"

"The song I'm writing for Tyler," said Mrs. Haggerty with a note of pride.

"You write songs?"

"First song I ever wrote. I used to give piano lessons, you know. But this song, I heard it rattling around inside my head, and I knew it was for Tyler. Don't you think it'll make a dandy Christmas present for him?"

Kelly started to answer, but before she could open her mouth, Mrs. Haggerty's fingers began to move across the piano keys. She sang her song, a little shakily perhaps, but her voice was on key, and the melody was really quite pretty.

"Do you suppose he'll like it?"

"Well, *I* like it! I wish I could play the piano like that."

A smile spread across Mrs. Haggerty's face. "Bless your heart. You sit down here next to this old lady." She patted the piano bench. "I'll teach you how to play."

Kelly had already taken piano lessons, and she hated them as much as she hated liver. Maybe more. But somehow, the way Mrs. Haggerty kept smiling and patting that piano bench, she decided to give it one more try. She sat down and put her right thumb on middle C. After Kelly played a few notes, Mrs. Haggerty shook her head.

Kelly stopped. "I told you I couldn't play."

"Nonsense. You can play."

"Well, what's wrong?"

"You're holding your hands too low," explained Mrs. Haggerty. "Are there mashed potatoes in your wrists?"

"Huh?"

"Hold 'em up. I tell you what, you just stay put and I'll be right back." She made her way to the kitchen and returned with a bag of peppermint candy.

"Hold your hands over the keys like little bridges. That's right." She placed a peppermint candy on the back of Kelly's wrists. "Now play," she ordered. "If the candy falls off, you're dropping your hands too much. If the candy stays on, you can keep it."

Kelly played and played. Before the afternoon was over, she had eaten five peppermint candies and had four more in her pocket. The grandfather clock struck six.

"I've got to go," she said. "If I'm not home in time for dinner, Ben'll eat my dessert."

"Do you have to hurry away?" Mrs. Haggerty followed Kelly to the front door.

"It's dark already!"

33

"Zip up your jacket. And for heaven's sake, don't forget your hat."

It wasn't until she was halfway home that Kelly realized that Mrs. Haggerty had forgotten to give her the four ninety-five again, and the list of names. She thought about Jennifer and Adelaide. What were they doing on a Sunday afternoon? Looking at all the prizes in the Bismarck Greeting Card Company prize catalog? Counting all their money?

She looked up at the first star of the evening, crossed her fingers, and made a wish. "I wish Jennifer would call me tonight at exactly eight o'clock."

5

The Camera Caper

Jennifer never called.

On Monday and Wednesday, Kelly had to stay late after school to rehearse for the sixth-grade play. The performance of *A Christmas Carol* was scheduled for the following Monday. Kelly had the part of the Ghost of Christmas Past.

On Thursday she and Ben went straight to Mrs. Tweel's house after they got off the school bus. Mrs. Tweel watched them from three thirty until five, when Mrs. McCoy returned from her job at Dr. Pratt's office.

On this particular Thursday, they dropped their books on the hall table and picked up the camera and tape recorder they had brought over earlier.

"How do you like it?" asked Mrs. Tweel. She held up Kelly's costume. Mrs. Tweel took in custom sewing projects and alterations for many people in Lawrenceburg.

Kelly examined the long white dress with the wide sash around the waist. Mrs. Tweel had sewn on pink, purple, and yellow flowers from shoulder to hem. "It's perfect!" cried Kelly. "I'll try it on in a little while. Right now, Ben and I have to go see Mrs. Haggerty."

Mrs. Tweel held the costume in front of Kelly and checked the length. "Must you go this minute?"

"It's very important, Mrs. Tweel. We're going to record Mrs. Haggerty's song with our tape recorder and take a picture of her, too. That way she can send her song and her picture to her son in Los Angeles. Don't you think that'll make a terrific Christmas present?"

"That sounds like a very good idea," said Mrs. Tweel.

"I wanna go, too!" called Samantha. She came home on the noon kindergarten bus and was glad to see Ben and Kelly when three thirty finally came.

"Not you, Sam," said Kelly. "We have important business to do."

Samantha's lower lip began to tremble, and tears came to her eyes. "Aw, please?"

Kelly smacked her forehead, exasperated. "Come on, then. But you better stay out of our way." She waved good-bye to Mrs. Tweel, closed the door, and turned to Ben. "How do you work this camera, anyway?"

"Just focus it," said Ben. "Right here. And don't forget to take a picture of the inside of that closet."

"What for?"

"Because if there *is* a ghost in there, it'll show up on the film. You can't see ghosts, but you can take pictures of them. I read all about it. They show up like white shadows in the picture. This will prove if the Haggerty house is haunted!"

36

"Are we going to a ghost house?" asked Samantha. She looked terrified.

"Of course not." Kelly turned to Ben with a scolding look and whispered, "Shhh! Be quiet. Samantha's gonna get scared."

"I'm not scared," said Samantha. "Mrs. Haggerty's nice."

"Yeah, she's all right," said Ben. "She keeps a man-eating barracuda in a fishbowl and a ghost locked up in her closet."

"What's a man-eating barracuda?" Samantha ran a little to keep up with them.

"It's just a goldfish. Don't worry," answered Kelly. She glared at Ben. "See what you did? You're scaring her."

They cut through the Gordens' backyard, walked across the frozen creek, and ran through another yard until they reached Stewart Street. Finally they stood at the bottom of the stone steps and stared up at the dark house.

"It does look haunted," said Samantha in a very small voice.

"It is!" whispered Ben. "There's a ghost locked in the closet. And there's another one that lives in the attic. The house is creeping with ghosts!"

"Don't listen to him," said Kelly. She gave her sister a push.

All at once, Samantha let out a wail that could be heard up and down Stewart Street. "Take me HOME! I wanna go HOME!"

"Terrific," said Kelly. "Now look what you've gone and done."

"Take me HOME!" Samantha stood as if her boots were frozen to the sidewalk. Kelly and Ben pulled her all

37

the way down Stewart Street, across the creek, and over to the Tweels' house.

She was still screaming when Mrs. Tweel came running to the door. "Samantha! What on earth happened? What's the trouble?"

"It's nothing," said Kelly. "Samantha just changed her mind. That's all." They quickly pushed Samantha inside and closed the door. A few minutes later, they stood on Mrs. Haggerty's porch.

"You *would* scare her half to death," muttered Kelly. She pressed the doorbell. "You and your man-eating barracuda."

"Well, there *is* a ghost in that closet!"

"Oh, Ben, there is not."

"Wanna bet?"

The door slowly opened. The biggest smile spread across Mrs. Haggerty's face when she saw Ben and Kelly. "Where have you been?" she scolded. "I've waited all week for you. Come on in, come on in." They hustled inside.

"I'm awful glad to see you. Here, hang your coats on the rack."

"We can't stay too long," said Kelly as she pulled off her jacket.

"I've got Cokes in the refrigerator. Now don't tell me you don't have time for a Coke." Mrs. Haggerty waved them toward the kitchen. "I was just having a little onion and garlic sandwich. Can I fix you one? Won't take but a jiffy."

"An onion and garlic sandwich?" Ben wrinkled his nose.

"Lordy, they're delicious and a heap better than all them fancy medicines those no-account doctors give you.

My throat's been acting up this week, and there's nothing better for a scratchy throat than a thick slice of onion sprinkled with lots of garlic on day-old bread. I'll fix you both one."

"Oh, no, thanks," said Kelly. "My throat's fine."

"I'll take a Coke," said Ben. "There's nothing better for my throat than a cold bottle of pop."

"Help yourself." Ben took a frosty Coke from the refrigerator, pried off the lid with a bottle opener, and gulped down half the bottle.

"What's that camera and tape recorder for?" asked Mrs. Haggerty.

"We wanted to take your picture," said Ben.

"And record your song," added Kelly.

"Whatever for?" Mrs. Haggerty sat back down at the table and bit into her onion and garlic sandwich.

"To send to Tyler," said Ben.

"We thought Tyler would like to have your song on tape and have a picture of you, too."

"Well, ain't that something," said Mrs. Haggerty. She chewed her sandwich and thought. "He'd like that. Yes, sir, he'd like that a lot. I wish my throat wasn't so scratchy. Scratches like a prickle bush."

"It'll be all right," said Kelly. Ben had already disappeared into the library. He began to play the piano and sing his favorite song, "Ninety-nine Bottles of Beer on the Wall." Mrs. Haggerty finished her sandwich and followed him in. Kelly gathered up the tape recorder and the camera and joined them.

"Do you know 'Chopsticks'?" asked Mrs. Haggerty. Ben pounded out "Chopsticks" and slid to the right of the piano bench as Mrs. Haggerty sat down. She joined in with a lower version of the tune, and together they nearly raised the roof, laughing and plunking away on the piano.

Kelly picked up the camera and snapped a picture of them. Then quickly, before she could change her mind, she crossed the hall into the parlor and reached for the knob on the closet door. The door swung open. She took a picture of the dark inside.

"How would you like to take piano lessons, young man?" Mrs. Haggerty asked Ben.

"Aw, I don't think so. I already know 'Chopsticks' and 'Ninety-nine Bottles of Beer on the Wall.' That's all I need to know."

"Well, you certainly can pound out a song."

"You're not bad yourself!"

Kelly plopped into the chair next to the piano. "I got a good picture of you, Mrs. Haggerty. Tyler should like it."

"You know, Kelly, I don't think I've given Tyler a picture in a long time." She peered into a mirror on the wall. "Now ain't I a sight?"

"He'll like the picture. I know he will," answered Kelly. "What do you think about singing your song now? I'd like to record it for him."

Mrs. Haggerty smiled as she played the opening chords of her song. Her voice filled the room as the tape recorder whirred.

> *He first saw California*
> *A long, long time ago.*
> *He traveled o'er the mountains*
> *And left us feelin' low.*
> *Feelin' low, feelin' low.*
> *He crossed those Rocky Mountains*
> *And left us feelin' low.*

"Keep the recorder going," whispered Ben.

"Why?"

"We might pick up some ghost sounds—wailing, rattling of chains, all that stuff."

"Good idea," said Kelly.

Mrs. Haggerty finished the song, stood up slowly, and turned around. "Before I forget, let me give you that four ninety-five. I have it here safe in my pocket." She reached into her pocket and handed Kelly the money.

At five o'clock, Ben and Kelly carried their camera and tape recorder back home. They crossed to the other side of Hopper Street when Kelly saw Adelaide and Jennifer building a snowman in Jennifer's front yard. The two girls talked together and pretended not to see Kelly, but she knew they were watching her.

"I've just saved a pile of money," Kelly told Ben. "Maybe I won't have to sell all those Christmas cards after all."

"Why not?"

"You're looking at two people who won't be getting any presents from me." Kelly jerked her thumb in the direction of Jennifer and Adelaide. "They're both creeps."

"CREEPS!" yelled Ben. Jennifer and Adelaide stopped packing snow on the snowman and turned around.

"I *was* going to get Jennifer a blue wallet with a unicorn on the front. She's always wanted one," whispered Kelly.

"Girls want the dumbest things."

"And I *was* going to get Adelaide a Super Pickle doll like that one hanging in the window of Lorey's. She likes to hang stuff around her room."

"SUPER PICKLE!" yelled Ben. Adelaide and Jennifer turned back to their snowman.

"Ben! Don't tell her!"

"Well, you said you weren't getting it."

"I'm not. They don't deserve anything!"

"What did they do, anyway?"

"It's what they didn't do. They didn't even wait for me so we could sell cards together. They took all the customers and left me with hardly anybody. And they think it's funny. They're just trying to make me mad. Running around doing everything together, leaving me out."

"That's terrible! I'd spread split pea soup all over their windows if I was you. Want me to help? We'll fix 'em!"

Kelly eyed Ben closely, almost considering the idea. She kicked a chunk of ice. "To think Jennifer used to be my best friend. If I'd known this was going to happen, I never would've asked Adelaide to be witches with us on Halloween."

"How 'bout putting stink cheese in their desks at school?" suggested Ben.

"Yeah."

"Or you could always pour glue in their gloves. I've tried that. It works great if they put 'em on before the glue dries."

"Hmmm."

Ben's face brightened. "Hey, I just thought of something."

"What?"

"With all the money you're saving, you could get me a telescope. I really like that one in your catalog."

"I'll tell you something, Ben. At the rate we're going, selling these dumb cards, we're not going to do *any* Christmas shopping! And we'll sure never be millionaires, either."

"Who needs a million dollars? All I want is that telescope."

6

Christmas Tree–Chopping Trip

On Sunday afternoon, the McCoys' van pulled up in front of Mrs. Haggerty's house. Mrs. McCoy, Ben, and Samantha waited as Kelly and her father went to get Mrs. Haggerty.

"Do you suppose we'll have any snow?" she asked as they helped her to the van. "I could swear a storm is coming. My bones are aching." A few snowflakes swirled through the air, but the sun shone brightly.

"It should be a perfect day for chopping down Christmas trees," said Kelly's father. "Almost all the snow has melted."

"What's in the bag, Mrs. Haggerty?" asked Samantha after everyone was settled in the van.

"This?" Mrs. Haggerty opened the bag. "Just a few apples. I thought we might get hungry going out in the woods like this, huntin' for a tree. Want one?"

Samantha smiled and reached for an apple. "Thanks!"

"Let's sing 'Jingle Bells,' " suggested Mrs. McCoy as the van pulled onto River Road. Mrs. Haggerty joined in. When the song ended, Kelly was surprised to see tears in her eyes. It was sort of hard to tell, considering the thick glasses that Mrs. Haggerty wore.

"This is mighty nice of you folks to take me out to hunt for a Christmas tree. We couldn't get one last year, what with Arthur feeling so poor. And we didn't have one the year before, either."

"How come?" asked Samantha.

"I guess when no one comes to visit, you just don't go to all the fuss and bother of puttin' up a tree."

"I'll come to visit," said Kelly.

"Me, too," said Ben.

"Well sir, I'd be proud if you'd all come. How about Christmas day? Arthur should be home by then, and we'll have some of my good eggnog and plum pudding. Wouldn't that be jolly?"

Mrs. McCoy turned around. "Are you sure you want *all* of us to come?"

"Sure I'm sure. Arthur will be pleased as punch to have some visitors. Now you've got to promise."

"All right." Kelly's mother laughed. "We'll come for a little while."

"Good!" said Mrs. Haggerty.

"How about 'Ninety-nine Bottles of Beer on the Wall'?" asked Ben.

"Please," said Dr. McCoy. "This is Christmas. We'll sing Christmas carols like we always do."

"Do we have to do everything like we always do?" grumbled Ben.

44

"It's tradition," said his father.

"Tradition," muttered Ben.

"How about 'It Came Upon the Midnight Clear'?" suggested Dr. McCoy. His tenor rang out and was soon joined by everyone. They sang one carol after another until they finally reached the Dillsboro turnoff.

Samantha pointed toward a small white farmhouse and a red barn that had MAIL POUCH painted on the side. "There it is, Dad. Stop!" The van pulled off the road and stopped in the gravel driveway of the Tulleys' farm.

Larry Tulley greeted them with a broad smile and pointed to the hundreds of evergreen trees that dotted the hillside. "Take your pick. Did you bring your hatchet this year, or do you want me to chop one down for you? I'll be glad to."

"We're chopping our own," said Ben, "the biggest one you've got."

"And one for Mrs. Haggerty," added Kelly.

Samantha tugged at Larry's jacket. "Before we get our tree, can I see the puppies?"

"Who said we have puppies?" Larry laughed.

"Aw, Larry, you always have puppies." Samantha tried to pull Larry toward the barn.

"Well, as a matter of fact, we do have a few pups. Come on, I'll show you." Larry led the way to the barn, shooing away a couple of chickens as he went. He opened the barn door and walked down the dirt path between the stalls. Stopping at the third stall, he pointed to a huge wooden box. "Now I don't know if Gertrude will like this or not, but I'll just reach in here and get one of these young critters." He pulled out a plump puppy that wiggled and

45

squirmed and whimpered as he handed it to Samantha.

"Oh, Mom, look. Can we take him home with us?" Samantha hugged the puppy.

Mrs. McCoy sighed. "I'm afraid not, Samantha. We've got two frogs and a skunk already. No dogs."

"Aw, Mom. Please?" begged Samantha.

"I'm afraid these pups are all spoken for," said Larry. "There won't be one left by Christmas Eve."

"Let me hold that rascal." Mrs. Haggerty took the brown and white spotted puppy from Samantha's arms and rubbed its warm head. "What kind is it?" she asked.

"It's a genuine mutt," said Larry. "Gertrude is mostly beagle. We have no idea who the father is."

"Well, it's the sweetest thing I ever laid eyes on." The puppy stuck out a little pink tongue and licked Mrs. Haggerty's cheek. She stroked his head a few moments more before handing him back to Larry.

"Say, Larry," said Kelly, looking around. "Where's Rufus?" Rufus was Larry's goose that had taken a bite out of her leg last winter. Kelly would never forget Rufus's sharp beak and loud honk.

"Rufus? He's around somewhere, getting into trouble. That crazy goose! I'll grab him if I see him," promised Larry. "Say, don't you kids want to ride the horses?"

"Yeah!" Kelly, Ben, and Samantha ran from the barn out into the bright sunlight and started across the pasture toward the fenced-in field.

"Look out," yelled Ben, pointing to Kelly's left. "Rufus!"

Kelly screamed and jumped to the right, smack into a smelly cow patty.

"Oh, Ben!" she cried.

But Ben was running behind Larry, laughing as hard as

he could. "Watch out for Rufus," he called, "and cow patties!"

Kelly scraped the stinking cow manure from her tennis shoes and ran after Larry. She tried to think of some way to get even with Ben.

The snow began to fall lightly as Kelly mounted Ginger, a sleek, brownish red horse with a black mane and tail. Ben and Samantha came along behind her on black speckled workhorses. Ginger stopped at the gate that opened into the pasture.

"What's wrong with Ginger?" yelled Ben. His speckled horse walked in a circle around Kelly's.

"Come on, Ginger," coaxed Kelly. "Let's go. You can do it. Giddap!" The horse slowly turned its head to the right. One big brown eye blinked at Kelly. Ginger didn't seem to be about to go anywhere.

"She won't move," complained Kelly. "She must have eaten a bowling ball." Ben leaned from his saddle and slapped Ginger sharply on her rump. The horse lurched forward as though stung by a bee.

"Hey!" yelled Kelly. "That's fast enough already. Help! Whoa, girl." Ginger raced through the gate opening, jumped a tree stump, and galloped toward the hillside.

"Larry! Help! How do you make her slow down?" Kelly arched back as much as she could and pulled on the reins, but Ginger had a mind of her own.

The horse galloped straight ahead, black mane and tail flying. Kelly spotted a large branch hanging low over the path. Before she could even think about it, she reached up and grabbed the branch, swinging free of the horse. She held on, legs dangling, until Larry rode up beside her, hooked her waist with his arm, and pulled her behind him onto his stallion.

"Am I glad to see you!" she shouted.

"Are you OK?"

"I think so," said Kelly, although she felt shaky all over.

"I can't imagine what got into Ginger. She never acts that way." Larry prodded his stallion toward the runaway and finally caught up with her. He reached for the loose reins, pulling the skittish horse to a slow trot. "Something sure spooked her."

"I know who the spook is around here—my dear little brother, Ben."

"Ben?"

"He slapped her rump. I saw him." Kelly held on tight to Larry's waist as they trotted back to the field.

"That was great, Kelly!" shouted Ben. "Boy, you sure got the good horse. How come you ran into that tree? Don't you know how to steer?"

"Very funny, Ben."

"Are you all right?" asked Mrs. McCoy. She checked Kelly from head to foot.

"I'm OK. Did you see me grab that branch? We'd have gone all the way to Timbuktu if that branch hadn't come along!"

"Let's get moving," called Dr. McCoy. "The sun's going down. If we want a tree, we'd better start looking."

Larry stayed with the horses while the McCoys and Mrs. Haggerty trudged across the pasture toward the hillside. "Can you make it, Mrs. Haggerty?" asked Kelly's mother. "Would you rather wait in the Tulleys' kitchen?"

"Lordy! What do you think I am, an old lady or something? I guess I've stomped around a farm or two in my day. I haven't had such a good time in a month of Sundays."

They both laughed and walked on. Mrs. Haggerty seemed more energetic than ever. She inspected one tree and then another. "Too big," she called as Kelly's father pointed to a long-needled pine. "Too lopsided. Too spindly," she said whenever anyone took an interest in a tree.

"Now here's a beauty," said Mrs. McCoy. She tilted her head to one side and studied a small white pine.

"Too crooked," stated Mrs. Haggerty, eyeing the tree through her thick glasses.

"I don't think so," said Mrs. McCoy. She walked clear around the tree.

"I like it," said Kelly.

"Great, here we go," said Kelly's father before anyone else could say anything. "Stand back!" He chopped down the tree with a few swings of the hatchet.

"Aw, Dad. That tree's too small," complained Ben. "Why do we always have to get such a short one?"

"Too late now," said his father. He dragged the tree behind him through the snow-covered hillside. "See anything you like?" he asked Mrs. Haggerty.

"Well sir, if you want to know the truth, these are the scrawniest little old trees I ever saw, but my bunions are acting up something fierce, so I'll settle for that spruce over yonder. What do you think?"

They all gathered around a small spruce tree. "It's perfect," said Kelly.

Mrs. Haggerty smiled. "Arthur will like it, won't he?"

"I'm sure he will."

"Chop it down!"

Dr. McCoy's hatchet sliced into the base of the spruce. "Timber!" yelled Ben as it toppled to the ground. Kelly and Ben dragged the spruce back to the van.

"Look out!" hollered Ben as he ran around Kelly and pointed behind her. "It's Rufus!"

"Yeah, I'm sure, Ben."

Rufus charged at Kelly's ankle with two loud honks and nipped her with his beak. "Ouch!" She spun around and saw the goose with its beak wide open. Rufus's eyes sparkled black.

"I've got him," yelled Larry, reaching for his goose. "Did he snap at you?"

"Yes!" cried Kelly. She rubbed her ankle.

"Don't say I didn't warn you," said Ben with a wide grin. "You ought to listen to me sometime."

Kelly lunged for Ben and almost grabbed his jacket, but he twisted out of her reach and took off running across the field. She thought about the school play scheduled for the next afternoon. How could she act in a play as the Ghost of Christmas Past with a broken ankle?

"Where's Samantha?" asked Kelly's father as he finished putting the trees into the van.

Mrs. McCoy gazed out across the field, shielding her eyes from the lowering sun. "Where *is* Samantha?"

"She was with us when we chopped down the tree," said Mrs. Haggerty.

"Sam!" cried Kelly.

"Samantha!" yelled Dr. McCoy.

They whistled and called and searched the farm, but Samantha had simply disappeared. "Think!" said Mrs. Haggerty. "Quit all this running around like crazy clowns at a circus. What would a girl like Samantha want to do on a farm like this?"

Everyone stopped.

"I know!" said Mrs. McCoy. "I bet she's in the barn."

"The puppies!" said Ben.

They hurried to the barn. Sure enough, in the third stall, curled up snugly next to Gertrude's box, was Samantha, fast aleep. A puppy nestled in her arms.

"Now ain't that a sight for sore eyes!" exclaimed Mrs. Haggerty. "All tuckered out."

"Wake up, Samantha. Time to go," said Dr. McCoy.

"I sure wish them hound dogs weren't all spoken for," said Mrs. Haggerty. "I wouldn't mind surprising Arthur with a little pup for Christmas. He's been talking 'bout getting a good watchdog. He sure would like one of these."

"Sorry. They're all taken," said Larry.

"Wake up, Sam," called Ben. He tickled her nose with a piece of straw.

7

Kelly's Costume Catastrophe

The morning of the long-awaited school play finally arrived. Kelly stood in front of the mirror in the family room and examined her costume. The dress, covered with pastel flowers, hung almost to the floor. As she turned her head, her white yarn wig swung left and right. She lifted her arms dramatically toward the ceiling and closed her eyes. "I am the Ghost of Christmas Past!"

"You look more like a bowl of spaghetti," said Ben. He sat at the kitchen table, spinning a bottle of Pepsi-Cola around and around.

"I am not a bowl of spaghetti. I am the Ghost of Christmas Past," said Kelly. She stepped into the kitchen and twirled on her toes in front of the refrigerator. Her long white skirt rippled into a flowing circle.

"More like the ghost of spaghetti past." He spun the Pepsi bottle faster.

"Ha ha, Ben. You should've tried out for the play. You probably could've gotten the part of Tiny Tim."

"Who wants to be in a stupid play? And have to dress up like a bowl of spaghetti? And memorize all those dumb lines? You think I'm nuts?"

"You really want to know?" asked Kelly.

"Oh, you ol' geezer SCRO-O-O-O-G-E!" sang Ben.

"*Ebenezer,* not 'you old geezer.' " Kelly rubbed her sore ankle where Rufus had taken a nibble.

"Let's get going, Kelly," called her mother from the bathroom. "You have exactly ten minutes until the bus comes. Take your costume off and put it in the bag. Make sure you fold it. Have you brushed your teeth yet?"

At just that moment, Ben opened the bottle of Pepsi with a can opener, and fizzy pop shot straight across the kitchen, hitting Kelly smack in the face. The pop splashed onto her yarn wig and dripped down her dress.

"Ben!" she screamed.

"Wow! Look what Ben did!" cried Samantha as Mrs. McCoy rushed into the kitchen. "He zapped Kelly!"

"I didn't mean to," said Ben. He hurried to the sink, picked up a sponge, and turned on the water. "That stuff *shot* out of the bottle, Mom. You should have seen it! I didn't do anything. I was just sitting there holding the bottle. FIZZ! WHAM!" Ben kept babbling on while he tried to sponge off Kelly's dress. He grabbed the ends of her drenched wig and twisted and squeezed as if he were wringing out a dirty mop.

"Mom!" cried Kelly.

Mrs. McCoy stood by the table, stunned. "This kitchen is an absolute disaster area," she finally managed to say. "And I have to be at work in twenty minutes. Oh, Ben!"

"I've got to have this costume today, Mom," said Kelly.

"Look at it. I can't wear this! I look more like a drenched sheep dog than the Ghost of Christmas Past."

Ben stood back and looked. "You know, you're right. You *do* look like a drenched sheep dog."

"Ben!" Kelly grabbed the sponge from his hand.

"Don't have a fit. Gee, it's just a little Pepsi. You'd think the ceiling just caved in or something."

"Oh, Mom, he's ruined it!" Kelly brushed Ben away. "He's ruined the whole play!"

"What a wild woman!" said Ben. He ran to the closet to get a mop.

"Take it off, Kelly, and put it in the bag," said her mother. "The wig, too. And then wash your face. Hurry!" Kelly's mother rushed to the telephone and dialed a number. "Ben," she said. "You're in trouble. I'm going to have a good talk with you tonight!"

"What did I do? Gosh, I didn't know that bottle was going to explode! FIZZ! WHAM! If Kelly hadn't been standing there, acting like the queen of the universe, she never would have got zapped with my superlaser machine."

"You should have seen it, Mom," said Samantha. "When that pop hit Kelly—ZAP—you should have seen her!"

"Go brush your teeth, Samantha."

"Oh, OK."

Mrs. McCoy quickly telephoned her friend. "Hello, Sylvia," she said. "I have a big favor to ask of you. Are you going to the play this afternoon at the school? Good. We have a small emergency here. Ben sprayed Pepsi all over Kelly's costume, and I have to be at work in fifteen minutes. . . ."

A half hour later, Kelly sat at her desk in Room 19 and

buried her face in her math book. She felt the stiff strands of hair in front of her ears. Short, straight hair was bad enough. But short, sticky, gooey hair was unheard of! And today of all days, the day of the school play. She wondered if she could sneak out and wash her hair in the girls' rest room.

The bell had not yet rung. She peeked over the top of her book as Jennifer and Adelaide strolled into the room. Together, as usual. They were always together. Her two best friends, and they completely ignored her. How could two people be so cheerful and friendly one week and so cruel and nasty the next? She thought about the Bismarck Greeting Cards and how they had ordered them from a catalog. The two of them, Jennifer and Kelly, as business partners, were going to be rich. Well, now Jennifer and Adelaide were rich, but Kelly had only sold four boxes. And she had lost two friends. It was a bad deal all around.

Kelly watched as Jennifer handed Adelaide a present wrapped in holiday wrapping paper and tied with a red bow. They talked and laughed together. Finally Adelaide reached into her schoolbag and pulled out a white box tied with a green ribbon.

"You have to wait until Christmas," Adelaide said.

"I can't! Come on, Adelaide. If I can open mine, then you can open yours. Please?" said Jennifer.

"OK. You first."

Kelly propped her book higher, but not so high that she couldn't see what was happening. Jennifer tugged at the ribbon and opened the box. She pulled out a blue wallet with a unicorn on the front. "Oh, Adelaide, I love it! This is just what I've been wanting." Jennifer laughed when she saw Adelaide's picture in the very first picture compartment. Beaming with pleasure, she opened and closed the Velcro fastener and passed it to Susan to look at.

Adelaide ripped the wrapping paper from her gift. She opened a box, and out onto her desk flopped a green Super Pickle doll, complete with a Super Pickle cape and dangling legs. Adelaide laughed so loud, Mrs. Ludlow looked up from her desk.

"Jennifer! You got me Super Pickle! How'd you ever know I wanted one of these? I love him!" Jennifer merely shrugged her shoulders and grinned.

How did she ever know? thought Kelly. *Because I told her that was exactly what Adelaide wanted. That was what I was going to get her.* Kelly felt the tears rushing to her eyes. She blinked hard, but it was no use. The tears streamed down her face, and she wiped them with the back of her hand.

Alex Bradford sauntered into the room carrying his Ebenezer Scrooge costume. A stovepipe hat perched precariously on his head. Alex *would* be Ebenezer Scrooge. Kelly pictured what she would look like four hours from now with gray makeup smeared on her face, black rings around her eyes, her wig like wet spaghetti noodles, her arms sticky with Pepsi, and her dress a dirty mess. Alex would probably think she was the ugliest girl at Riverview.

He walked down the aisle and snapped his finger on the back of her math book. "How's it going?"

"Oh, hi, Alex!"

"You been crying?"

"Crying?"

"Yeah, crying."

Kelly rubbed her eyes. "I have an onion sandwich in my desk. That's all."

57

"An onion sandwich? Are you crazy? Since when do you like onion sandwiches?"

"Uh, since today. I like to try something new every day."

"Really? You ought to try radishes with peanut butter. Now that is good."

"It is? I'll try that tomorrow."

"Say, what'd you do to your hair?"

Kelly felt her face growing hot. "My hair?" She touched the sticky hair on her forehead. "I squeezed something on it. Some kind of mousse or something."

"You squeezed a moose on your hair?"

"Sure. It's the latest thing, Alex. Mousse in a jar."

"You got a moose in a jar? I don't believe it."

"They sell it at the drugstore, Alex. You squeeze the mousse on your hair and rub it in."

"Now that's gross," he said. "Squeezing moose stuff on your hair. Ugh." He started to go to his seat. Kelly covered her head with her book. He stopped and pulled her book back. "But you know what?"

"What?"

"I like it." He pulled a strand of her hair.

"You do?"

"Yeah. You look like one of those punk rockers. Wild."

"You think so?"

"Too bad your ghostie wig will cover it. Where's the wig?"

"It's at home. Mrs. Malone's bringing it down later."

"Who's she?"

"One of Mom's friends. She lives on Stewart Street."

"Isn't your mom coming?" Alex asked.

"She might, if she can get off work for an hour. I sure hope she makes it."

58

The bell rang, and Alex tipped his stovepipe hat to Kelly, winked, and slid into his seat. Kelly closed her eyes. Alex was definitely the cutest and the nicest boy in the entire school. The only trouble was, everyone else thought so, too.

At twelve thirty, Kelly was biting her thumbnail. She paced to and fro backstage, whispering her lines and sneaking glimpses of the gym now and then as it filled with parents and younger students. Oh please, Mom, she thought. Please come this minute and bring my costume.

Everyone else was already in costume, and the teachers and students in charge of makeup were scurrying about in the room across the hall from the stage. "Kelly!" called Mrs. Ludlow. "For pity's sake, put on your costume! We're about to begin."

"Mrs. Ludlow," said Kelly, swallowing hard. "I think I'm going to be sick."

"You can't be. Not now."

"I'm going to be."

"You're just nervous, that's all." Mrs. Ludlow took Kelly's hand and patted it. "Hurry, now, and get dressed."

"I can't remember any of my lines. Not one! I think I'm going to be sick."

"Listen, Kelly. You're not sick! There's no time to be sick. You'll be just fine. You'll see."

"I'm sick."

"Where is your costume?"

"It's at home. My brother sprayed a bottle of Pepsi all over it this morning."

"What?" Mrs. Ludlow shrieked. Kelly looked up, surprised. She had never heard Mrs. Ludlow shriek quite so loudly.

"He got it in my hair, too. Feel this."

Mrs. Ludlow looked at her watch. "Get on your makeup and stay calm. Stay calm. Everything's going to be just fine. I'll go hunt up an old sheet or something."

"Five more minutes," hollered Amanda as Kelly hurried into the dressing room. "Where's your costume?"

"My skunk ate it," said Kelly. She dipped her hand into a container of gray grease and spread it across her cheeks. Then she drew two black rings around her eyes.

"You look more like a raccoon than a ghost," said Amanda. "Here, let me help."

"Well, I've never seen a ghost. How should I know what they look like?"

"Kelly! Kelly McCoy!" Kelly jerked her head around. The lipstick in Amanda's hand made a long red streak across Kelly's cheek. Rushing through the doorway came Mrs. Malone, waving the ghost costume in her hand. Mrs. Haggerty came along behind her, holding the white yarn wig.

"Sorry we're late," said Mrs. Malone. She leaned over Kelly and whispered quickly. "I called Mrs. Haggerty this morning and mentioned the play. She absolutely insisted that I bring her along. She said she wanted to see you."

"I hope I don't forget my lines," said Kelly.

"Mercy me!" gasped Mrs. Haggerty when she finally caught sight of Kelly. "Is that you? You look . . . strange."

"Ghostly, you mean." She gave Mrs. Haggerty a quick hug. "I'm supposed to be a ghost." Kelly pulled on her wig and stepped into her dress. "Ghosts aren't supposed to be gorgeous."

"We'd better get a seat," said Mrs. Malone as she took Mrs. Haggerty's arm. "Break a leg!"

"Thanks!"

Ten minutes later, when Kelly stepped out onto the stage, she scanned the audience for her parents. She spotted Ben, sitting with the fourth graders, but she could not find her parents anywhere. Didn't Dad say he was coming for the evening performance? And Mom probably couldn't get off work. It was odd, her mother not being there. Before she had gotten her job at Dr. Pratt's office, Mrs. McCoy had come to every Christmas program, ever since kindergarten days. Now she wasn't there.

As Kelly moved slowly across the stage toward Ebenezer Scrooge, she glanced again at the audience and found Mrs. Malone and Mrs. Haggerty, sitting on the left side of the gym. Mrs. Haggerty smiled and waved her hand. Kelly pretended not to see her, but she couldn't help smiling just a little. Eighty years old, and Mrs. Haggerty had come all the way to Riverview School to see her.

Jennifer and Adelaide, finished with their ushering job, sat in the front row and whispered behind cupped hands. Kelly wondered if maybe they were just a little bit jealous. After all, it wasn't every girl who was lucky enough to be on stage with the cutest boy in the sixth grade. Maybe *that* was the reason they were sticking together like two halves of a Popsicle and leaving her out.

The Ghost of Christmas Past stood directly beside Ebenezer Scrooge. Alex stared at the top of Kelly's head and made strange noises between his teeth. He looked worried. She tilted her head sideways, trying to figure out what the trouble was. Her yarn wig slid off onto the floor. She grabbed it and put it back on. Alex pressed his lips together and squinched his eyes closed, trying very hard not to laugh. Kelly could not remember her next line at all.

8

The Secret Staircase

"We need help," called Ben to his good friend Buster Gorden as he, Kelly, and Samantha left Mrs. Tweel's house two days later and plodded through the backyards to Stewart Street. Buster, who was a bit on the chubby side, looked like a snowman all bundled up in his jacket, ski pants, and boots. He had spent the past few days building a snow fort in his backyard, but now there was not enough good snow to work with.

"Where are you going?" he hollered.

"We're gonna help Mrs. Haggerty put up her Christmas tree," called Ben.

"Who's Mrs. Haggerty?" asked Buster.

"You know. That old lady who lives in the spook house over on Stewart—the one who hands out candied apples and nickels," replied Ben.

63

"The house Ernie was chicken to go to?"

"That's it. Come on and help us."

Buster placed a snowball on top of a stack of snowballs and hurried to join his friends. Soon the four of them stood at the bottom of the steps to the Haggerty house.

"Something tells me this place *is* haunted. Look at it!" said Buster.

"Shhh." Kelly put her finger to her lips. She noticed Samantha's face turn a shade of gray.

Samantha looked up at the long icicles that hung from the gutters. "I think I want to go home."

"Not again," moaned Kelly.

Ben leaned over to Buster and whispered, "There's something weird about the closet in the front room. The door slammed shut the other day. Kelly almost jumped a foot in the air."

"Slammed shut? All by itself?" shouted Buster.

"What's all by itself?" asked Samantha.

"Uh . . . this house," answered Ben. "It's standing here . . . all by itself. Isn't that something?"

"Well, I'm not afraid," said Kelly. "Mrs. Haggerty promised us cookies if we help her with her tree. Now let's go!" They climbed the steps and found the spruce tree on the porch, just where they had left it Sunday.

The door opened, and there stood Mrs. Haggerty in a long cotton dress and a gray shawl. She smiled broadly when she saw the Hopper Street kids.

"This is Buster," said Ben.

Mrs. Haggerty leaned forward to get a close look at Buster. "Well, I can't say as I remember you, young man. Hmmm. Could you be that rabbit that comes around every Halloween?"

"Rabbit? I was never a rabbit! I was a warlock."

"Warlock. Well, of course. I'm happy to meet you." She shook hands with Buster.

"You want us to bring in this tree?" asked Ben.

"I wish you would. I have the very spot for it. Come on in."

Ben and Buster pulled the tree through the hallway and into the library, following Mrs. Haggerty. They set it down beside the piano, next to a window.

"There. That'll do. Can you lift it into this stand?"

Between Kelly and Buster and Ben, the spruce tree was lifted and placed into a metal stand and turned both left and right until Mrs. Haggerty held up her hand and said, "Stop right there! I want it just like that." They all stood back and admired it.

"I have something I want you to see," said Mrs. Haggerty. "It's a tree skirt I made years and years ago." She spread a red circle of felt on the floor. Appliquéd and hand-embroidered in very fine stitches were Santa Claus and his sleigh, a snowman, a stocking, a wreath, a star, a church, a nutcracker, a candle, and an ice skater.

It was the most wonderful Christmas tree skirt Kelly had ever seen. She touched the sparkling sequins of the candle and the shiny gold braid of the snowman's scarf. "Did you really make this?" she asked.

"I made each little figure," said Mrs. Haggerty as she stroked the old red felt. "Tyler always loved this little church. He likes these sequin windows. Aren't they pretty?"

"Yeah!" all four said with a note of awe.

"Who's Tyler?" asked Buster.

"My son."

Kelly studied the sequin windows. "You know, they look like colored-glass windows. This is beautiful."

"Thank you." Mrs. Haggerty beamed with pleasure and pulled the tree skirt a bit closer. "And Arthur, he's most fond of the nutcracker. See?" Mrs. Haggerty pointed to a red and blue soldier. "Arthur always takes me to *The Nutcracker Suite*—the Christmas ballet at Music Hall." She sighed. "I suppose we'll have to miss it this year."

Kelly touched the sequined soldier. "How is Mr. Haggerty?"

"He's much better. He should be getting out of the hospital by next Tuesday or Wednesday. Oh, my, what a fine Christmas we'll have, with Arthur back home, and you folks visiting, and this wonderful Christmas tree."

"I can't wait!" said Ben.

Samantha picked up Mrs. Haggerty's book of poems by Robert Frost and opened it to page 1. "What's this?" she asked.

"Put that down, Samantha," scolded Kelly. "That book is special. Tyler gave it to Mrs. Haggerty last year."

"I get a hankerin' now and then to hear a good poem." Mrs. Haggerty sat down on the settee. "But if you want the truth, I can't even read it."

"What?" said Buster. "You don't know how to read?"

She looked up and chuckled. "Of course I know how to read. Used to read all the time. I loved to read. But with these old eyes, I can't make out all the fine print anymore. I don't know why they have to use that itty-bitty print. A body needs a magnifying glass to see it!"

"I'll read it," said Kelly. "What poem do you want to hear?"

The old woman leaned her head back and closed her eyes. " 'A Time To Talk,' " she said softly.

Kelly searched the index and opened the book to page 156. She read:

> When a friend calls to me from the road
> And slows his horse to a meaning walk,
> I don't stand still and look around
> On all the hills I haven't hoed,
> And shout from where I am, "What is it?"
> No, not as there is a time to talk.
> I thrust my hoe in the mellow ground,
> Blade-end up and five feet tall,
> And plod: I go up to the stone wall
> For a friendly visit.

"Man, I never can understand that poetry stuff," said Buster, scratching his head.

"I got it," said Ben. "You're supposed to play and have a good time instead of working all the time. Right?"

Mrs. Haggerty smiled at Ben. "I think what Mr. Frost is saying is that we ought to talk to our friends when we have the chance. We'll always have work to do, that's a fact. But we won't always have friends, not unless we talk to them now and then."

"Mrs. Haggerty has a hundred friends," Ben told Buster. "She's giving us a list of names so we can sell all Kelly's Christmas cards, as soon as she finds the list. Right, Mrs. Haggerty?"

Mrs. Haggerty frowned. "I declare, I haven't found that list yet, have I?" She started to get up, but Kelly waved her hand.

"It's too late, Mrs. Haggerty," she said. "Don't worry about your list. I sent that box of cards back to the Bismarck Greeting Card Company. I'm not the salesman type. I hate selling stuff."

67

"You did?" said Ben. "Why didn't you give it to me? I could have sold them."

"Nobody buys cards this close to Christmas," grumbled Kelly. She slowly closed the book. Mrs. Haggerty's words echoed inside her head. "We'll always have work to do, that's a fact. But we won't always have friends, not unless we talk to them now and then." Kelly thought about Jennifer and Adelaide. She hardly talked to them anymore at all.

Buster sniffed the air. "Mmmm! What smells so good?"

"That's my plum pudding," answered Mrs. Haggerty. "I made it this morning just so you young'uns could have a piece when you popped in." She stood up slowly and walked into the kitchen. "It's still a-simmerin'. Won't be long now, though."

Kelly breathed in the wonderful, warm, sweet smells of raspberries, oranges, apples, lemons, raisins, currants, cinnamon, ginger, and nutmeg. "Gosh, I wish my mom could make plum pudding," she said.

"Look!" Samantha ran to the kitchen table. Lined up in neat little rows were snowman cookies. With coconut faces and pink frosting hats, they stared up at her with dark raisin eyes.

"Oh, can I have one?" begged Samantha. "Please?"

"Well, sweet thing, I made them for you." Mrs. Haggerty ruffled Samantha's hair. "I don't know who else would eat them if you don't. But leave some for Arthur. What would he think if he came home and didn't get one of his favorite cookies, hmm?"

They all reached for one. The sugar cookie melted in Kelly's mouth. She crunched on the coconut and licked the pink hat. "You're a super cookie baker!" She tried to picture Jennifer and Adelaide at that moment. Were they baking Christmas cookies, too? Were they punching out the dough with cookie cutters and putting them in Jennifer's oven? Were they pouring out glasses of milk and eating the cookies as fast as they scraped them onto the wax paper, just like she and Jennifer had done last year?

"Where are your tree decorations?" asked Ben. "We better decorate that tree before it gets dark. We've got to be home on time tonight. We're having pizza."

"Tree decorations," repeated Mrs. Haggerty, looking flustered. "Oh, yes! I remember where they are. Up in the attic beside the trunk. They're in a cardboard box."

"The attic?" said Buster. His eyes grew large. The cookie he was bringing to his mouth stopped in midair. He gulped.

"You have to take the secret stairway," explained Mrs. Haggerty. She walked to the corner of the kitchen and opened a narrow wooden door. "Right up these stairs. This will let you out in a bedroom. If you turn right, there's another door that opens to the second stairway. That one goes straight up to the attic."

Buster popped the cookie into his mouth, chewed it quickly, and swallowed it. "I think I'll stay here," he mumbled.

"I think you'll come with us," said Kelly. She pulled him toward the door.

"I have to go to the bathroom," said Buster.

"You do not," said Ben.

"Tyler used to sleep in that bedroom," continued Mrs. Haggerty. "He always came down to breakfast through this stairway instead of the main stairs. He said it was more fun."

Kelly carefully stepped into the dark passageway. Ben and Buster followed her, single file, and Samantha came last.

"I don't want to be last!" cried Samantha when the door swung shut. The stairs, in total darkness, were so narrow that no one could pass anybody.

"It's cold in here," said Ben. "Hurry up."

"Quit poking me," said Kelly. "How would you like to go first? I can't see a thing."

"Are you sure this old house isn't haunted?" asked Buster. "Are you sure there are no ghosts in here?"

"Aaaah!" Samantha wailed.

"Don't say that word, Buster," warned Kelly. She tripped on a step and scrambled back up.

"What word—*haunted*?"

"No, *ghosts*. Just don't say it, OK?" Kelly swiped at the cobwebs that hung loosely in delicate strands. "You ought to be glad you're not first. I'm getting tangled up in all these sticky cobwebs."

"Spider webs!" said Ben. "And they're probably crawling with hairy spiders. Thousand-leggers. Tarantulas."

"Ben!" screamed Kelly. Something brushed her cheek. She stumbled up the last step and burst through the door into Tyler's old bedroom. A large ceramic panther crouched at the foot of the bed, as though ready to pounce. On an oak dresser stood a model of a tall pirate ship.

"Wow! I could go for a room like this." Ben reached for the panther.

"Don't touch anything," said Kelly. She picked cobwebs from her hair.

"Why not?"

"Because this is Tyler's room, not yours."

"Aw, Kelly."

70

"And look at all the dust," she continued. "I think we should help clean this place."

"This house is just too big for two old people to take care of," said Ben.

"What if they decide to move?" said Buster. "To an apartment or something?"

"Then they'll move," said Kelly weakly. She didn't want the Haggertys to move. Mrs. Haggerty was a sweet old lady—not at all an old bag, like Adelaide had said. She was . . . a real friend, even though she was eighty years old and couldn't see very well.

"You guys go on up," said Buster. "I have to go to the bathroom." He turned to go.

"Oh no, you don't," said Ben. "We're sticking together." He pushed Buster toward the second door.

Kelly opened it and gave Buster a shove. "In you go."

"Not me!" cried Buster. He shrank back. "I'm not going first. I'm not crazy."

"*I'll* go first," said Ben. "I'm the only one here who's not a big scaredy-cat."

"Ha!" laughed Kelly. "You're afraid of monsters hiding under your bed at night."

"I am not."

"You are, too."

They entered the second staircase and gripped the railings as they made their way slowly upward. "Listen," whispered Buster. "Shhh! I hear something." He stopped. Kelly bumped into him. Samantha bumped into her.

"What is it?" asked Samantha, clutching Kelly's jeans pocket.

"Shhh!"

They all held their breath and listened to the creaking of the steps under their feet.

"I don't hear anything," said Kelly, "except my heart pounding like crazy. Go! Go!" She pushed Buster. They all dashed up the last few steps and banged open the attic door.

A musty smell hit them as they burst into the attic. With the bit of light that came through a small window at one end, Kelly, Ben, Buster, and Samantha were able to see the huge, low-ceilinged room filled with boxes, suitcases, wardrobes, chairs, lamps, toys, and other odds and ends that the Haggertys had collected over the years. Kelly brushed past a dusty black box, shaped long and low, sort of like a coffin. She jumped back. Samantha ran to a hobbyhorse whose mane and tail flew in the breezeless room.

She clambered onto the horse and bounced up and down, squeaking the rusty springs noisily, while Buster made funny faces in a cracked mirror. Ben opened the lid of a trunk and held up an old navy uniform.

"Wonder who this belongs to. Tyler?"

"Come on, you guys. Quit touching everything. I mean it," said Kelly. "Let's get those decorations and get out of here. This place gives me the creeps."

She grabbed the uniform from Ben's hand, tried to fold it, and finally laid it carefully back in the trunk. After closing the lid, she started searching through the cardboard boxes beside the trunk. She pushed aside one with dishes and opened another. Old piano music. She pushed it back.

"Mrs. Haggerty said the decorations were beside the trunk, didn't she?" Kelly spun around. "Didn't she?' Her voice echoed in the stillness. The squeaking of the hobbyhorse had stopped. The attic was as quiet as a tomb. Not a sound. And no sign of Buster, or Ben, or Samantha. They were gone. They had simply vanished, it seemed, into the dust.

Kelly jerked around and stared at the mysterious long box. A rusty hinge squeaked as the lid moved ever so slightly. Slowly, so slowly that Kelly thought her heart would burst, the lid began to rise. *This is it,* she thought. *The end. Here I am in an attic all alone. And something is about to rise up from that black box. Something or someone.*

9

Ghost Crazy

"Boo!" said Samantha. She pushed the lid straight up from the box and poked her head over the side.

"Oh my gosh, Sam. Don't ever do that again! You almost scared me out of my wits." Kelly's heart pounded wildly. "Where'd Ben and Buster go?"

"I don't know. They told me to get inside this dumb box and say *boo* when you opened it. I got tired of waiting. I don't like this box." Samantha climbed out. She was covered with dust and dirt.

A bat suddenly swooped down from a niche in the wall and swept by Kelly's ear. She ducked. It circled the attic twice and was soon joined by another one. "Birds!" cried Samantha.

"Bats, you mean! We're getting out of here this minute! Decorations or no decorations. Come on." Kelly grabbed

Samantha's hand and pulled her toward the attic stairway. The door swung closed behind them, enveloping them in darkness. "Careful now, don't fall," Kelly warned. She stepped down the wooden stairs, gripping the railing as she went. "There ought to be a light in here."

"Wait for me!" cried Samantha.

"Those dumb boys. They sneaked off and left us up there all by ourselves." Kelly tripped and fell down the last two steps, against the door to Tyler's bedroom. She jumped up and twisted the doorknob. It wouldn't open.

"Darn, I wish I had a flashlight." She twisted the doorknob again. "Very funny, Ben. Open up!" she called. "I know you're in there." Samantha held Kelly around her waist and cried. "Come on, Sam, quiet down. I'm trying to listen. I think they're hiding in Tyler's room." Samantha sniffed and tried hard to keep quiet.

"Shhh!" Kelly heard footsteps above them. The feet slowly stepped across the attic floor toward the stairway.

"I knew it! They were hiding in the attic all along," she whispered. The attic door creaked open and closed, and Kelly climbed up two steps and then stopped. The sound of footsteps descending the steep stairway, step by step, could be heard, coming closer and closer.

Kelly's heart seemed to stop beating as she realized that such dragging footsteps did not belong to Ben. Or Buster. Then she heard it. A strange, heavy breathing sound. Deep, loud, raspy breathing.

"Ben!" she screamed. She pounded her fists on the door. "Open up! Buster! Mrs. Haggerty! Open the door! Please!" The door flew open.

"Gosh! You sound like a wild woman! You want to

wake all the mice?" Ben laughed until tears rolled down his cheeks. "We only left you for a minute! Were you scared?" He wiped his face with the back of his hand. Kelly and Samantha whisked into the bedroom and slammed the door behind them.

"Where's Buster?" asked Kelly.

"He had to go to the bathroom," answered Ben. "What's the matter with you anyway? You look like you've seen a ghost."

"We did! Th-there's someone in there," stammered Kelly.

Samantha buried her face in Kelly's sweatshirt and clung to her with both arms. "Huh?"

"Shhh! Listen!" Kelly turned slightly and pressed her ear to the door. Ben stopped talking and listened.

"I don't hear anything," he said after about ten seconds. "What are you talking about?"

"There's someone in there!" said Kelly. "We heard him, didn't we, Samantha?"

Samantha only squeezed closer to Kelly and trembled from head to toe.

Ben pulled Kelly from the door. "Let's see."

"No, Ben!" cried Kelly. "You open that door, and it'll be the end of us!"

"Me? Afraid? Watch this." He reached for the doorknob.

"Ben! Please don't open that door!" begged Kelly. She covered her mouth with both hands but could not cover her eyes as Ben yanked the door open. They peered into the dark staircase.

"You know what?" said Ben. "I think you're ghost crazy! There's nothing in here."

"Yes, there is," insisted Kelly as she peeked over Ben's shoulder. "I heard footsteps. And breathing—loud, horrible breathing. Oh, Ben, it was awful!"

"I think you ate too many coconut cookies," said Ben. "Your head's turning into a coconut." He knocked on her head with his knuckles. "Hollow."

"Ben!"

"You're hearing things that aren't even there."

"OK, *you* go up and get those decorations, then," said Kelly.

"Ghost crazy," said Ben. "Ha, ha, ha! Look out, here comes the ghost. He's going to get us. W-O-O-O-O!"

"EEEEYAAAAAOO!" All of a sudden, a bloodcurdling scream ripped loose from the dark staircase. Buster pounded down the steps like a raging lion, roaring, growling, and finally leaping, arms outstretched, into the bedroom. He stood hunched forward, arms over his head, fingers curled. "The ghost of the attic is here!"

"Buster!" Kelly clutched Samantha to her side. "I should have known!"

Buster and Ben doubled over with laughter. "Did you really think he was a ghost?" said Ben when he was able to talk. "Didn't you know it was Buster?"

"W-o-o-o-o!" sang Buster.

"One of these days, Ben McCoy," said Kelly, "the trick is going to be on you. You just wait and see. Come on, Samantha." She opened the door to the lower stairway and pulled Samantha behind her into the corridor. Ben and Buster followed behind, laughing and pushing, all the way down the steps and into the bright, sweet-smelling kitchen.

"I was afraid you'd gotten lost," said Mrs. Haggerty. She bent over a cardboard box filled to the brim with colorful balls and pinecones and decorations of every sort.

Kelly stared at the box. "I thought that box was in the attic."

"I thought so, too," admitted Mrs. Haggerty. "But after you left, I remembered where I put it. It was in the cabinet out in the pantry." She shook her head. "I can't remember where anything is these days."

"I sure wish you'd remembered before we went up there!" said Kelly. "Your attic is a very spooky place, Mrs. Haggerty."

"It is?"

"Yes! Did you know you've got bats up there? Hundreds of them all over the place." Kelly paused. "Well, at least two."

The old woman only rubbed her chin with a thin hand. "Well, of course there are bats in the attic. Don't all attics have bats? They've been up there for years. There's no getting rid of them. Might as well just live with them."

"I think you've got bats in *your* attic," said Ben to Kelly. He tapped his finger on his forehead. "Come on, wild woman, let's decorate the tree." He carried the box of decorations to the library.

After circling the tree with the cord of colored lights, the children and Mrs. Haggerty hung glass balls of red, blue, and green. Then came angels, elves, and all sorts of wooden handmade decorations.

"I like this little drummer boy," said Samantha. She pointed to a hand-painted drummer boy that twirled among the branches.

Mrs. Haggerty set a large bowl of popcorn on top of the piano. "That little drummer boy has been beating that drum for years. Tyler made me that when he was about your age."

79

Buster reached for the popcorn. "Go ahead. Help yourself," she said, "but leave a few for the popcorn chain." She disappeared into the kitchen and brought back a bowl of cranberries.

"Now, young lady," she said to Samantha as she handed her a large needle and a spool of white thread, "I hear you're a humdinger of a popcorn stringer."

"I am!"

Kelly and Samantha busied themselves stringing cranberries and popcorn while Ben, Buster, and Mrs. Haggerty hung more decorations.

The doorbell rang. "I'll get it," Kelly called. She ran to open the front door.

Malvina Krebs and her daughter, Marigold, stood on the porch, bundled up in winter coats and scarves against the cold wind. Malvina lived across the street from Kelly and always kept a close eye on anything happening in the neighborhood. A few days before, Samantha had told Marigold all about the horrible haunted house on Stewart Street, the man-eating barracuda that Mrs. Haggerty kept, and the ghost in the closet. Marigold had told her mother, and Malvina Krebs, as usual, decided to investigate.

"Hi, Marigold!" shouted Samantha. "Look at my popcorn chain. We've got cranberries, too." She held up the chain for her friend to see.

"Where's the man-eating barracuda?" asked Marigold. "I wanna see it."

Mrs. Haggerty was all smiles as she greeted Mrs. Krebs and Marigold. She insisted that they take off their coats and join in the tree trimming.

"Let me get you a cup of hot tea," said Mrs. Haggerty.

"Can't stay but a minute," said Mrs. Krebs. "I only came to ask you a question." She looked all around the library from ceiling to floor and even poked her head into the kitchen. She frowned and sniffed the air. "Do I smell something burning?"

"That's my plum pudding. Care for a piece? It's delicious."

"I do!" said Marigold. Kelly helped Mrs. Haggerty cut the steaming pudding and fill the plates.

"I always put brandy in mine," said Mrs. Krebs. "And applesauce." She took a bite and chewed slowly, as though trying to decide whether to compliment the cook or not. "Hmmm. This is delicious!"

"Have some more."

"No, no. No more, thank you." Malvina Krebs sat up very straight and prepared to say something of great importance. "Mrs. Haggerty, I've come to ask you a question. Have you ever heard about the séances I hold every Thursday afternoon?"

"One of them Tupperware parties?"

Mrs. Krebs lowered her squeaky voice to a whisper, which only made Kelly lean closer and listen all the more. "A séance is a meeting where people get together in order to communicate with the spirits."

"Communicate with what spirits?"

"Those who have died and gone on before us. We call them back. They come into the room where we sit, and they talk to us." Malvina Krebs tapped her skinny fingers on the kitchen table. "For the past few months, we haven't been very successful. I think it's my house, or maybe we should hold the séance in the evening, after dark. Yes! The vibrations would be better in the evening."

"I declare, I've never in my born days heard tell of such a thing," said Mrs. Haggerty. "You hold one of those whatcha-ma-callit meetings every Thursday?"

81

"Every Thursday." Malvina cleared her throat. "I was wondering if you would like to hold the séance tomorrow, here in your home."

"Here?"

"This house is perfect." Malvina Krebs looked all about the room and nodded her head up and down. "It has such strong vibrations. The conditions couldn't be better. Oh please, Mrs. Haggerty, what do you say?"

"My land! I'll have to tidy up the place. I'll have to—"

"Wonderful!" cried Malvina. She jumped to her feet and grasped Mrs. Haggerty's hand. "We'll be here at seven o'clock. I'll bring the candles. Oh, and I'll bring my carrot cake and my coffeepot. You won't need to do a thing." She slipped into her coat and went to search for Marigold.

"Can I come, too?" asked Kelly. She had never been to a séance before.

"You?" said Mrs. Krebs. She peered down her long nose at Kelly. "Hmmm. Well, I see no reason why not. As long as you follow the rules."

"Oh, I will. I promise!"

After Mrs. Krebs and Marigold left, Kelly draped her popcorn-and-cranberry chain among the upper branches of the tree. Samantha hung hers below. Ben stretched on tiptoe and placed the tinsel star at the top.

"Perfect!" said Kelly.

"Won't Arthur be surprised?" Mrs. Haggerty clasped her hands under her chin and gazed with pleasure at the Christmas tree. Kelly plugged in the lights, and they all stood back. No one said a word as the magic filled the room.

10

Phantom Face

"Aren't you a little young to be attending one of Malvina's séances?" asked Kelly's mother.

"Come on, Mom, I'm eleven years old! Please?" said Kelly.

"Do you really want to go?"

"Yes!"

"All right, Kelly. But make sure you come straight home."

"Thanks!"

"What if you see a real live ghost?" Kelly's father chuckled as he picked up the *Register*. "O-o-o-o-o!" he moaned eerily.

The word *ghost* sent a shiver up Kelly's spine. "Don't worry, if I see a ghost, I'll holler *boo!*" She laughed. But deep inside, she trembled with excitement. It was fun going to Mrs. Haggerty's house. She knew it wasn't *really* haunted, but it certainly was an interesting place. When she was there, she didn't have time to worry about Jennifer or Adelaide—about how they never called or talked to her in school anymore. Mrs. Haggerty wasn't a bit like them. She was always happy to see her.

"I guess I'll go work on my pen collection," said Ben. He opened his mouth wide, yawned, and then tromped up the stairs.

Within minutes, Kelly was on her way to the séance. Through the dark yards she ran, between the bare trees crusted with ice. A cold breeze whipped the pine trees and scattered a few dead leaves. Snow was beginning to fall as she climbed the steps of the Stewart Street house. It loomed dark and foreboding in the cold December evening. Gray clouds passed swiftly behind it as Kelly looked up at the small attic window. She would *never* go into the attic again!

Malvina Krebs opened the door, quickly introduced Kelly to the guests, and directed her to take a seat in the cozy parlor. A warm fire crackled in the fireplace. The scent of the spruce tree filled the room with a rich evergreen smell. Mrs. Krebs had definitely taken charge of the whole affair and instructed everybody how to position their chairs in a close circle around the walnut table. The fishbowl was gone. In its place stood one purple candle, surrounded with a ring of red berries and shiny green leaves.

Kelly was introduced to Mr. Gunkleheim, a nervous old man who kept shuffling his shoes under his chair; Mrs. Heller, who nodded and smiled at her as though she had never seen a child before; Mr. Murray, a tall man with a gray beard who worked at the Shell gas station; Mrs. Katonis, the widow from Dillard Avenue; and Mrs. Farley, a mountain of a woman who continually stole glances at the carrot cake and plum pudding on the dining-room table.

"What do we do next?" asked Mrs. Haggerty. She was enjoying herself.

"I believe the mood will be right," said Mrs. Krebs, "if we sing a few songs. Chester?"

Chester Gunkleheim rose from his chair and strode, straight-backed and serious, to the piano in the library. Everyone followed behind him like ducklings trailing a mother duck. Without saying a word, he sat down at the piano, stretched his fingers, and began to play one song after another. They all joined in singing, the words being well known to everyone except Kelly and Mrs. Haggerty.

Mrs. Farley stood erect with her hands clasped in front of her. She sang out like an opera star. Mr. Murray bellowed as loudly as Mrs. Farley, but completely off-key. No one seemed to mind. Mrs. Katonis had a high, piping voice that sounded like a canary. Poor Mrs. Heller developed a bad case of hiccups during the very first song. She tried to swallow them but only succeeded in making them worse. Kelly held Mrs. Haggerty's hand, and the two of them hummed along and sang the words whenever they could. Mrs. Krebs was the song leader. She watched first one person and then another as she swung her arms in the air, keeping the rhythm. With each passing song, enthusiasm grew and filled the room until suddenly Malvina Krebs raised her left hand, closed her eyes, and tilted her face upward.

"I believe we are ready. The vibrations are right."

"I vow, those were mighty fine foot-stompin' songs, weren't they?" said Mrs. Haggerty. "Let's sing another one."

"Please! We must have total silence." Malvina spoke with authority. She walked back to the parlor and stirred the logs in the fireplace until the flames shot up. "Everyone take your place." She flipped the light switch and threw the parlor into darkness except for the yellow glow cast from the flickering flames in the fireplace. Long, dark shadows danced on the walls behind the sitters. She struck a match, lit the purple candle, and sat back down.

Mrs. Heller hiccuped.

"You know, a dose of vinegar and sugar for those hiccups would do you a world of good," said Mrs. Haggerty. "Cures them every—"

"Ahem! We must have total silence," repeated Mrs. Krebs with a scolding glance. "Now then, everyone please join hands." When Kelly saw the sitters stretch their hands, palms down, onto the round table, each person hooking a little finger to the one sitting nearest, she quickly did the same. She hooked fingers with Mrs. Farley on her right and Malvina Krebs on her left.

"Who are we to contact tonight?" asked Mr. Murray.

"My great-grandmother," said Mrs. Heller. "Great-grandmother Esmond passed away fifty years ago. She ate some bad huckleberry preserves. At least that's what—*hic*—"

"Name, please?"

"Rose."

"Rose, Rose, Rose, Rose, Rose," repeated Mrs. Krebs. She began to rock and swing in her seat, chanting the name of Rose Esmond over and over until the whole group seemed hypnotized. Kelly heard a sound like a bird flying into the windowpane.

"She is here!" cried Mrs. Krebs. Everyone turned toward the window. Behind the sheer white curtains, a face seemed to rise up and hover for a few seconds in midair. Kelly's heart skipped a beat. She stared at the phantom face floating in the darkness. Was it real? She couldn't believe her eyes. But there it was—eyes, nose, and mouth. Everything else was too hazy to make out. She pulled her hands away from Malvina's and Mrs. Farley's and rubbed her eyes.

The face at the window faded away. Snow fell, thicker and faster. "Great-grandmother Esmond—hic—!" called Mrs. Heller. "Come back! I have so many—hic—questions for you." The more excited she grew, the worse her hiccups became.

"Rose! Rose!" called Malvina. But the face was gone. Suddenly Kelly wished she had never come. This would be impossible to explain to anyone at school. And her parents would never believe her. Jennifer would, though. She knew Jennifer would believe. She longed to see Jennifer and Adelaide. She decided then and there that she would call them first thing in the morning. Maybe tonight. It wasn't too late. Someone had to make the first move. If they wouldn't, she would. They couldn't stay mad at each other forever.

"Name, please?" repeated Malvina. She closed her eyes once again.

"Agatha!" called Mr. Gunkleheim. "I want to call Agatha."

"Agatha, Agatha, Agatha," chanted Malvina Krebs. Soon everyone, including Kelly and Mrs. Haggerty, joined in the chant. A rustling was heard at the window, and when they all turned to look, once again a mysterious face materialized from nowhere. It bobbed up and down, left and right, as though it wanted to come right through the window but didn't know how.

"Agatha!" cried Mr. Gunkleheim.

Mrs. Heller hiccuped.

"As I live and breathe!" exclaimed Mrs. Haggerty. "I ain't seen nothin' like this on TV!" Slowly the phantom drifted away into the night.

The séance only lasted one hour. By eight o'clock, Kelly was running down the front steps as fast as she could go. She ran all the way home without stopping and burst through the front door.

"How was it?" asked her mother. Ben bounded down the stairway, two at a time.

"Fabulous!" Kelly tried to catch her breath. "We saw two ghosts! Two! We really did!"

"Oh, yeah? Were they by the window?" asked Ben.

"Yeah, right by . . . Wait a minute. How did you know?"

Ben couldn't contain himself any longer. He exploded with laughter, only stopping now and then to let out a long *BOOOO!* From behind the TV he finally pulled a wooden yardstick. On the end of the stick was glued a white construction-paper face, complete with crayoned eyes, nose, and mouth.

"Boy, I can fool you every time!" he said.

"Ben!" scolded Mrs. McCoy.

"You probably scared those poor séance people to death," said Dr. McCoy. He tried very hard not to smile. "When did you slip out, anyway?"

"I just tiptoed out," answered Ben. "You should have seen them, Dad. They were staring at that window like King Kong was climbing through it or something. That one guy's eyes were as big as pizzas. It was really good."

"That was you all the time?" asked Kelly. "There weren't any ghosts?"

"Nope. Just Buster. He's the one that bumped into the window and almost broke it when he tripped over a bush."

"You ruined the whole séance, Ben," grumbled Kelly. "You probably kept the real ghosts away. How could a real ghost come with a weirdo like you messing around outside?"

"Who's a weirdo?" Ben howled with laughter. "You were the one jumping up and down in your seat. I thought you were gonna bust your chair. No joke!" He put both fists up in front of his face and danced around, jabbing at the air. "Wanna arm wrestle?"

"Not with you," said Kelly. She started down the basement stairs to her bedroom. "If I were you, Ben, I'd close your curtain tonight. A *real* ghost just might be outside your window."

11

Frosty Frolics

Late that night, Lawrenceburg, Indiana, was hit with the worst storm of the winter so far. Strong winds bent the trees outside the McCoys' house, although Kelly slept snug in her basement bedroom, unaware of winter's fury. By the time she ran upstairs for breakfast, the world outside was buried beneath seven inches of snow. Branches, yesterday bare, now drooped under billowy coats of white.

"Call time and temperature!" said Ben.

Kelly dialed the number. The friendly girl from American State Bank said, "Time, seven-ten. Temperature, eighteen."

"Wow, that's cold!" Kelly reached for the radio dials and tuned in WSCH. Samantha and Ben joined her beside the radio as the announcer read a list of school closings.

"Oh, please, please, please, please," Ben prayed, squeezing his eyes closed, tilting his head upward, and pressing his palms together.

"The following schools are closed: Milan schools, South Dearborn schools, Lawrenceburg community schools—"

"That's us!" hollered Ben.

"Hurray!" They flipped off the radio and danced around the kitchen in a circle, holding hands.

"Now I can make some money for our shopping trip," said Ben.

"How?" asked Kelly.

"Shoveling snow."

"You?"

"I can shovel snow! Take a look at these muscles. Go on, feel this. Solid iron!"

Kelly squeezed Ben's arm and laughed. "Solid Jell-O."

"Wanna arm wrestle?" asked Ben. "I'll show you."

"'Fraid not, squirt."

"You know I'd win, that's why," said Ben.

"Go away."

"You're just jealous 'cause you're a girl. No muscles. That's your problem."

Kelly dropped to the floor. "OK, Ben. You're on."

Ben stretched out on the floor, grasped Kelly's hand, and pushed with all his might. His eyes were pinched tight, his face turned red, and his cheeks were about to explode. His arm, however, bent slowly to the right until it touched the floor. "Jell-O," said Kelly with a grin.

"You just wait. I'll take you on again next month. Mom! Can you fix me a big steak for breakfast? And spinach. I need spinach. And maybe a pepperoni pizza with lots of cheese. OK, Mom? I'm hungry!"

"It's pancakes, today, Ben." Kelly's mother flipped

some pancakes from the skillet onto a platter. "Looks like Christmas vacation starts one day early this year."

"And not one day too soon," stated Kelly.

"I'll miss our party!" Samantha suddenly realized that this was the day of the kindergarten Christmas party. "We should have had it yesterday."

"You children be good for Mrs. Tweel today. Hurry on over there after breakfast."

"Aw, Mom." Ben twirled his fork around on his plate.

"Can't you stay home today?" asked Kelly.

"I want you to pull me on my sled," said Samantha.

"I wish I could." Mrs. McCoy tickled Samantha under her chin. "I'll be off next week, though. I'll pull you on your sled then."

"Promise?"

"I promise. And we'll go shopping, too. OK?"

"If we're not snowed in," said Kelly. She ate three fluffy pancakes with warm maple syrup dripping down the sides, drank two glasses of orange juice, and stood up. "I think I'll shovel snow, too."

"Who's on dishes?" asked Mrs. McCoy.

"Samantha is," said Ben. He got up quickly.

"Kelly is," said Samantha. She pointed a sticky finger at Kelly.

"Ben is," said Kelly. "I'm sure of it. I did them yesterday."

"Oh, nuts," grumbled Ben. "You would have the world's best memory. You ought to be in the *Guinness Book of World Records*—best memory and ugliest face in the whole world!"

"Ben!" Mrs. McCoy gave him a stern look.

"Only kidding, Mom. Don't worry. I'll do the dishes."

In a few minutes, after the dishes were finished, Kelly, Ben, and Samantha searched the closet for their gloves. "I'm going to shovel Mrs. Haggerty's sidewalk," said Ben. "It's humongous."

"Hey, let me help!" Kelly pulled on her gloves. "We'll do it together and get it done in half the time."

"And have to split the money, too," said Ben, thinking it over.

Kelly thought of Mrs. Haggerty, alone in her big house with her goldfish and her television set. "I don't know, Ben. Maybe we should shovel her sidewalk for free. She's been really nice to us, you know."

"Free? Are you kidding? I'll never get to be a millionaire if I work all the time for free. I sure can't get rich off my skimpy allowance." He looked sideways at his mother.

"There are more important things than making money," said Kelly.

"Yeah? What?"

"Well, friends for one thing. I think I'd rather have one good friend than ten thousand dollars. I mean a really good friend. One who likes me a lot."

"You're nuts. I'd take ten thousand dollars any day!" Ben tugged hard on a stubborn boot. "There's no way I'm going Christmas shopping unless I shovel some sidewalks today. I'm down to the bottom of my bank—enough to buy a half of a candy bar."

"Frankly," said Mrs. McCoy, "you don't need to spend a penny on me. All I want is your love—a great big hug and a kiss, and maybe a whole day with no bickering or fighting. That would be the best Christmas present ever. I mean it."

"Oh, Mom," said Ben. "You can't *hold* love. I want to

get you something you can hold. Like a hamster or something."

Mrs. McCoy reached over and gave Ben a hug. "Honestly, Ben, all I want is your love. Whatever you do, don't get me a hamster."

"A box of love." Samantha giggled. "You'd open it and there wouldn't be anything in it!"

"If you can't hold it, what good is it?" asked Ben.

"It's the thought," said Mrs. McCoy.

An hour later, Hopper Street was buzzing with activity. Was there anything better than a day off from school, seven inches of new snow, and Christmas only six days away? Marigold and Samantha flopped down on their backs and made snow angels in the Tweels' front yard. Buster built his fort one foot taller and stacked a pile of snowballs higher, just in case someone should make the foolish mistake of walking into his yard. Ben quickly gave up the idea of snow shoveling when he saw Buster. Soon the two of them were in the middle of a blinding snowball fight.

Kelly cut through the yards, ducking between snowballs that flew from Buster's fort. She held her snow shovel up as a shield and ran until she reached Stewart Street. Walking through the deep snow, she thought about Jennifer and Adelaide. She had called Jennifer after breakfast, but she wasn't home. Adelaide wasn't home either. She thought about calling Amanda, another girl in her class. Amanda lived so far away, though. And Rae Jean had just moved to Ohio. She had barely gotten to know Rae Jean.

She stopped. There stood the old Haggerty house, its gingerbread trim frosted with snow icing. And who had beat her to the snow-shoveling job? Jennifer and Adelaide!

Of course they weren't at home. They were out shoveling snow together. Always together. The two of them heaved snow over their shoulders while they talked.

"I always seem to be a little late," interrupted Kelly.

"Oh, hi, Kelly!" called Jennifer. "Where've you been all week?"

"Around."

"Want to help us?" asked Adelaide. "We're only doing one more. Then we're going over to Jennifer's to—"

"Adelaide!" cried Jennifer. She slapped her mittened hand across Adelaide's mouth and whispered into her ear with her back to Kelly.

"I'd rather shovel snow by myself," said Kelly. She wasn't sure if she was going to cry or not. She picked up a handful of snow, pressed it into a ball, and flung it toward the telephone pole. It hit with a *thud,* leaving a circle of white on the dark pole. "Anyway, Mrs. Haggerty and I have a lot of important things to do today."

"You're always over here," complained Adelaide.

"Sure I am," answered Kelly. "We have all sorts of good things to do."

"Really?"

"That's all right, Adelaide," said Jennifer. "Remember?"

"What?"

Jennifer quickly whispered into Adelaide's ear. "Oh, yeah!" said Adelaide with a grin. "I almost forgot." She dug her shovel into the snow and pushed.

"We'll see you tomorrow, Kelly," said Jennifer.

"Sure," said Kelly. She was about to go on to the next house with her snow shovel when she heard Mrs. Haggerty calling. She looked up at the porch. Jennifer and

Adelaide could spend from now 'til Christmas together. She had Mrs. Haggerty—her own special friend.

"I was going to tell you a secret," Kelly called over her shoulder.

"Yeah? What?" asked Jennifer.

Kelly thought about how she was helping Mrs. Haggerty fix up the huge old house, decorating it for Christmas. She thought of the cookies and the plum pudding and the beautiful spruce tree in the library and how pleased Mr. Haggerty would be when he came home from the hospital.

"I'm not telling." They certainly had their secrets. She could have one, too.

Mrs. Haggerty held out her hand. "Come on in. No sense in dillydallying out here on such a blustery day," she said when Kelly reached the porch. "Want a Coke? I've got Cokes in the refrigerator. You just help yourself."

"Thanks."

"Aren't those two girls your friends?" Mrs. Haggerty motioned toward Jennifer and Adelaide. "Do you suppose they'd like a Coke, too?"

"They're no friends of mine," said Kelly. "Not anymore." She walked into the front hall and took off her jacket. "Friends don't run around whispering in front of you. They don't tell secrets and leave you out. They don't do things together unless they include you, too, do they? Would *your* friends do that?" By this time, Kelly had reached the refrigerator. She pulled out a Coke and opened it.

"Oh, maybe. Friends don't always act like they should."

"You're lucky," said Kelly. "You've got a hundred

friends. I wish I had a hundred! That way, if two acted stupid, I'd still have ninety-eight others."

"Not so lucky. My friends are just about all gone."

"Huh?" Kelly looked up from her Coke. "But you told me . . ."

Mrs. Haggerty sighed. "When you get old like me, your friends dwindle away, one by one. But I do have Arthur, and Mrs. Heller, and Sophie out in Iowa. I get nice letters from Sophie now and then. 'Course, I have a dickens of a time reading them. You ought to see how pinched up Sophie writes."

Mrs. Haggerty walked into the parlor and sat down in the rocking chair by the fireplace. She leaned her head against the back of the chair and heaved a deep sigh. Kelly followed her in and sat cross-legged on the floor in front of the fire. On the table nearby lay the copy of Robert Frost's poetry. The fire was so warm, and Mrs. Haggerty seemed so weary. Kelly decided to forget the snow shoveling, at least for a while.

"Would you like me to read you a poem while I'm here?" she asked.

Mrs. Haggerty's face wrinkled into a smile. She opened her eyes. "Oh my, I'd like that. I'd like that ever so much. My poor old eyes ain't what they used to be."

Kelly suddenly knew what she would get Mrs. Haggerty for Christmas! She would buy it Monday, if they weren't snowed in. She sat on the floor by the rocking chair and opened the book of poetry.

"Say, how would you like to go shopping with us Monday? Mom's off work and we're going downtown, to Cincinnati."

"Mercy, no, I'd only slow you young folks down."

"Oh, please! Don't you want to see the giant nutcracker on Fountain Square?"

"I haven't been to town in ages."

"Then you should come. We'll see the lights and everything!"

Mrs. Haggerty thought a moment. "I do need to get Arthur a warm housecoat."

"Great. I'll tell Mom."

"Are you sure she won't mind?"

"Mom? Naw!"

12

Cincinnati, December 22

"This is right nice of you folks," said Mrs. Haggerty. She sat bundled up in her green coat in the McCoys' van. Her white hair was tucked neatly under a small black hat.

"We won't stay long," said Kelly's mother. "I have a few last-minute items to get. That's all. And Ben wants to see the trains."

"Me, too," said Samantha.

"I only have two dollars and thirty-five cents," grumbled Ben. "What can I get for two dollars and thirty-five cents? I need a raise, Mom. When's the last time I got a raise?"

Kelly counted the money in her purse once again. Exactly eleven dollars and forty-three cents. "You should've shoveled snow last Friday. You'd be rich."

"I didn't have time. Buster and I had a wild snowball fight. I plastered him."

"Aren't we there yet?" asked Samantha.

"Not long now," said her mother. They had already crossed the Ohio-Indiana state line and were headed east down River Road to Cincinnati.

"How about loaning me a dollar since you're so rich?" Ben asked Kelly.

"Nope. I need it all."

"I'll pay you back."

"Nope."

"Fifty cents? Come on, Kelly. A hamster must cost at least three dollars."

"I don't want a hamster," said Mrs. McCoy.

"I'll get one for Dad," said Ben. "Everyone likes hamsters, Mom. You've got to be the only person in the whole world who wouldn't love to find a cute little hamster running around the Christmas tree on Christmas morning. I'd love one! I'd name him Homer the Hamster and get one of those hamster cages with the spinning wheel inside for him to play with. Gosh, this'll be the best Christmas present Dad ever got! Come on, Kelly, loan me a dollar. I'll pay you interest."

"I said NO!"

"Please, Mrs. Rich Bank President of the First National Bank? Can't you spare a dime for a poor boy like me?" Ben held out both hands.

Kelly hummed a sad song as she pretended to play a violin.

"Thanks a lot." Ben stuck his tongue out at her, wiggled his fingers by his ears, and made all sorts of ugly faces.

"What's wrong, monkeyface? Someone steal your banana?"

"Kelly!" said her mother. "Stop talking like that."

"Well, look at him, Mom."

Mrs. McCoy glanced in the rearview mirror at Ben, who sat straight up, his eyebrows raised, his mouth spread in a wide grin.

"Behave yourself, Kelly. I told you I wanted you children to give me one day without any fighting. That's all I want for Christmas."

"I thought you wanted love," said Ben. "I've got plenty of love. But no fighting? With a sister like her? Come on, Mom, that's impossible!"

"I could do it if I didn't have him for a brother," Kelly said. "He starts it all."

"I do not." Ben grabbed Kelly's hat and tossed it in the back of the van.

A few minutes later, the van circled Fountain Square. Kelly gazed at the tall red and blue nutcracker, just like the toy soldier in the ballet she had seen at Music Hall. He stood towering over the trees on the square. In the growing darkness of the late afternoon, the trees, twinkling with hundreds of tiny white lights, looked like a diamond forest over which the huge wooden soldier kept watch.

They drove to the Cincinnati Gas and Electric Building on Fourth Street and parked in front. Inside, trains of all different kinds chugged around and around a huge oval track. Some rattled across bridges. Some sped through tunnels. Kelly held her breath as two trains headed toward each other. Just as a crash seemed about to occur, one train switched onto a new track, while the second disappeared into a dark tunnel.

In a little while, everyone piled back into the van and drove to the Westin Hotel. Samantha giggled with delight as they came out of the revolving doors into the grand foyer. The entire room was aglow with Christmas lights. Dozens of animated figures, dressed in nineteenth-century style, worked to raise a multicolored hot-air balloon from the snow-covered ground. It was all make-believe, Kelly knew, but it seemed so real. The balloon puffed up and billowed out, smiling children skated on the frozen pond, dogs scampered in the snow. Mrs. Haggerty walked around the colorful display, pointing at one thing and then another. Her face beamed with delight as much as Samantha's.

"Can we look in the toy shop?" asked Kelly. The toy shop was inside the hotel just around the corner from the animated winter scene. Kelly pointed to the window, which was alive with dolls from every land, exotic stuffed animals, dancing marionettes, and moving trucks and cars. She could have gazed at that window for hours.

She noticed Ben recounting his money. "Here, Ben." She opened her purse, pulled out a dollar, and handed it to him with a smile. "You owe me one dollar, plus interest."

He looked up and grinned. "Thanks!"

"We have a few minutes," said Kelly's mother as she helped Mrs. Haggerty toward the toy shop.

When Kelly saw a tiny straw basket swinging from a blue and yellow striped balloon, she couldn't help but think of Adelaide. Adelaide loved to hang things from her ceiling, anything from handmade mobiles to fancy dolls. Kelly knew she would love it. "I'll take it," she told the clerk.

The minute she held the basket and balloon in her hand, she knew that she must get a gift for Jennifer, too. As rotten as they had been, she could not let Christmas go by without giving them each a present.

Kelly searched for something Jennifer would like that didn't cost too much. She had to have money left over for Mom and Dad, Ben, and Samantha. And of course, she wanted to get a special present for Mrs. Haggerty.

Her eye was caught by a box of pins that stood beside the cash register. They were metallic pink with purple unicorns painted on them. Kelly remembered how Jennifer had wished for a unicorn a few years earlier. She still wore a T-shirt with a unicorn on the front and drew unicorns on all her notebooks. Kelly knew she would like that pin.

She tried to picture Jennifer and Adelaide opening their presents. Even if they didn't get her anything, and she knew they wouldn't, she still wanted to see their faces when they opened her gifts. She didn't want to fight anymore. After all, it was December 22, almost Christmas Eve. Nobody should be angry on Christmas Eve. A warm feeling of happiness crept over her as she paid for the pin.

By the time they stopped in the candy shop next door, and made a few more purchases at Elder-Beerman across the street, they were ready to head back to Lawrenceburg. They walked out of Elder-Beerman onto Vine Street. Shoppers hurried left and right. Two magnificent horses pulling a black buggy came to a stop directly in front of them, their warm breath puffing white clouds into the night air.

"Would you look at this!" exclaimed Mrs. Haggerty. She clutched the shopping bag that contained the new housecoat for Arthur. "I haven't been in a buggy for years.

When I was a girl, Kelly, like you, my papa used to drive us up and down the countryside on Sunday afternoons in a buggy just like this one."

"Let's go for a buggy ride!" cried Samantha.

"Yeah!" called Kelly and Ben.

Mrs. McCoy laughed. "I'm sure Mrs. Haggerty is far too tired for a horse-and-buggy ride. It's getting quite late."

"Horsefeathers!" answered Mrs. Haggerty. "I want to see if this young man knows how to drive one of these things!"

"OK," said Mrs. McCoy. "Let's go!"

They all helped Mrs. Haggerty into the seat next to the driver. Kelly squeezed in beside her, and Ben and Samantha hopped in the backseat with their mother. "Giddap!" shouted the driver as he flipped the reins. The two black horses tossed back their heads and shook their manes in the breeze as they *clomp-clomp*ed noisily along the pavement. Cars and buses carefully made way for them.

Samantha waved to the people as the buggy rolled along Vine Street, past the nutcracker guarding Fountain Square. Shoppers smiled and waved back at them in a happy holiday spirit. "Let's sing 'Rudolph the Red-Nosed Reindeer'!" Samantha started to sing and was soon joined by Kelly and Ben. By the time the horses turned onto Sixth Street, everyone was singing, even the driver, who certainly had a redder nose than Rudolph after being outside all day.

After the ride had ended, Kelly held Mrs. Haggerty's hand as they walked back to the van.

"Mrs. Haggerty?"

"Hmm?"

"Do you think I could borrow your poetry book—you know—that one by Robert Frost?"

Mrs. Haggerty looked surprised. "My book?"

"See, I have this project I'm working on, and I need a good book of poems. I won't keep it long."

"Keep it as long as you want. I can't read it anymore."

"I'll give it back soon, I promise."

"Did I tell you my boy, Tyler, got me that book?"

"Uh-huh, you did."

"He forgets how up in years his mother is. See all these pretty Christmas lights?" She stopped walking and pointed to all the lights—the traffic lights, store windows, headlights, signs, Christmas lights decorating the lamp-posts, and all the hundreds of lights in the trees. "You don't see them like I do. When your eyes are as bad as mine, you see swirls of colors. Everything all melts together like a drippy ice-cream sundae."

Kelly squinched her eyes together and tried to make all the lights melt together into a giant ice-cream sundae, but she couldn't do it.

13

Christmas Countdown

On December 24, Kelly and Ben watched the antique clock on the mantel and counted how many more hours until they could go to bed and dream about Christmas. "Eleven more hours," moaned Kelly. "I'll never make it."

She poured cereal into a bowl on the floor. Her skunk, Cinnamon, nibbled at it. Ben was busy trying to tie red ribbons around his frogs' necks. Samantha was sorting out all the ribbons from the ribbon box.

All of a sudden the front door blew open, and in stomped Dr. McCoy. "That is some wind! I think it's getting ready to blow up a blizzard." He unzipped his jacket and pulled out a wiggling brown and white puppy. "What do you think of this? I got your friend Mrs. Haggerty a present."

"Dad!" exclaimed Kelly. She ran to the puppy and

scooped him up in her arms. "How did you ever get him?"

"From Larry. Someone changed his mind, and he had this one pup left over." Kelly's father scratched the puppy behind the ears. "As I recall, this little Fido was practically all Mrs. Haggerty talked about on the way back from Larry's farm last week. Remember?"

"Oh, Ben, look at him!" Kelly giggled as the puppy licked her face and wagged his tail as hard as he could. "This is the very one Mrs. Haggerty was holding. She's going to love him!"

"I want him!" said Ben.

"Not this one, Ben," said Dr. McCoy. "This one's for Mrs. Haggerty, if she wants him."

"She will," said Kelly.

"But Dad—" cried Ben. He plopped Fritzi and Mitzi back into their cardboard box and shoved the box behind a chair.

"Sorry, Ben. Maybe next summer. You can wait, can't you?" asked his father.

"No."

"Yes, you can. Mrs. Haggerty said her husband's been wanting a good watchdog."

"We can help take care of him, can't we, Dad?" asked Samantha.

"Sure."

"Hey, that's a good idea!" said Kelly. "I'll take him for walks every day, and you can feed him."

"What do I get to do?" asked Ben.

"You can . . . clean up after him."

"You mean . . . ? Forget it!"

"Oh, and I picked up our pictures at the drugstore," added Dr. McCoy. He laid an envelope of pictures on the lamp table. "A couple of them turned out sort of blurry. But the rest are good." Her father went back to the van to get a few more things, and Kelly quickly opened the envelope. She skipped over the pictures of Samantha and the van and the Thanksgiving turkey and stopped when she saw the pictures of Ben and Mrs. Haggerty and the mysterious closet.

"Ben, look at this." Ben and Samantha were chasing the puppy underneath the kitchen table and into the family room. "Ben, come here. Take a look!"

"What?"

"Look at this picture. What's this white, shadowy smudge in the closet?"

"What smudge? What closet?" Ben studied the picture closely. "Is this the picture you took?"

"Yes! What do you think? See any ghost?"

"Are you kidding? I don't see anything! Why didn't you focus the camera? I told you to focus."

"I thought I did."

"Wait a minute," said Ben. He held the picture of the closet upside down and sideways. "You know, I think this *is* a ghost! I *do* see a smudge. Look!"

"You think so?"

"Let's show this to Mrs. Haggerty," said Ben. "She'll flip her dentures out if she knows there's a ghost in her closet."

"Let's not. There's no ghost in this dumb picture. There's no such thing as ghosts." Kelly snatched the picture from Ben's hand and ripped it in half.

"Hey!" yelled Ben. "You just tore up the evidence!"

Kelly looked at the picture of Mrs. Haggerty playing the piano with Ben. "This one's a lot better. Tyler will like this one."

Samantha walked into the kitchen carrying the squirming puppy. "Let's go over to Mrs. Haggerty's now. I get to carry the puppy."

A few minutes later, they climbed the stairs to the old house on Stewart Street. The wind was blowing so hard that a sudden gust whipped Ben's hat from his head, and he had to chase it across the yard and halfway down the street. Mrs. Haggerty's face brightened when she saw them. But something was wrong.

"Arthur's not coming home tomorrow," she said as she walked back into the parlor. A soap opera was playing on the TV.

"Oh, Mrs. Haggerty, why not?" they all asked practically in unison. They gently placed the cardboard box with the puppy on the hall floor and followed Mrs. Haggerty into the parlor.

"That doctor of his called me on the telephone yesterday morning and said something about his medication not being quite right yet. They want to keep him for a few more days. Maybe a week." She picked up her handkerchief and blew her nose. "I miss him so much."

"Well," said Kelly. She tried to think of something cheerful to say. "He'll be home in a few days. A few days isn't much time."

But Mrs. Haggerty seemed miles away in thought. "And Tyler. I want to see Tyler."

"Look." Kelly handed Mrs. Haggerty the picture of her and Ben at the piano. "I'm really sorry it took so long to get these pictures developed. At least you sent Tyler the tape of your song last week. I bet he has it by now."

"I sent him a long letter, too," added Mrs. Haggerty. "I'll write him another one today and put this picture inside."

111

"It's a little blurry," said Ben. "I should've taken it."

Mrs. Haggerty looked down at the picture and smiled. "Just look at that. Oh, Tyler will like this."

"And we got you a present," said Samantha. She couldn't wait to tell about the puppy. Samantha loved secrets, but this one she could keep no longer.

"You did?"

"We sure did!" said Kelly. "Wait 'til you see this." She and Ben and Samantha carried the box into the parlor, lifted the lid, and pulled back the blanket. The puppy opened its sleepy eyes and trembled in the corner of the box.

"Glory be!" Mrs. Haggerty lifted the shivering puppy from the box and held it to her cheek. She touched the smooth, round top of the puppy's head.

"Larry had one puppy left over that nobody wanted," explained Ben.

"Nobody wanted?" cried the old woman. "Did nobody want you?" She held up the spotted puppy and laughed. "Well, somebody wants you now, bless your little heart. You need a good sweater. Look at you just a-shiverin' and shakin'." She almost forgot the children were there as she began to croon to her new baby, cuddling him in her arms.

"Can we help take care of him?" asked Samantha. "Please?"

"Sure you can! The first thing we'll do is knit this little fellow a new sweater. Can you knit?"

"No," said Samantha.

"Well, it's high time you learned." The puppy licked Mrs. Haggerty's hand as she held him on her lap. "I've got an idea! Let's have a party—to celebrate!"

"A party?" Samantha tilted her head sideways, puzzled.

112

"Now?" asked Kelly.

"Why not? It's early. You can invite your friends, and I'll get the hot dogs and marshmallows. Yes, sir, we'll have a grand old picnic!"

"But, Mrs. Haggerty," said Kelly. "This is the day before Christmas. Did you forget?"

"I know that. But I'm sick and tired of that television! Who says we can't have a little party? We'll have a picnic right here on Christmas Eve, just like the ones we had when I was a girl."

"We can't have a picnic," said Kelly. "It's freezing outside."

"Not outside. Inside! Right here by the fire. A winter picnic."

"I love picnics!" said Samantha.

"With hot dogs and marshmallows. All right!" shouted Ben.

Kelly shrugged her shoulders. "I never heard of such a thing, but it sure sounds like fun." She was really glad to stay. A day spent with Mrs. Haggerty always passed so quickly. Before she knew it, it would be the long-awaited night before Christmas. She thought about Jennifer and Adelaide. She had just finished wrapping their gifts and had planned to call them that afternoon.

"Say, Mrs. Haggerty. Could I invite Jennifer and Adelaide?"

"Jennifer? Adelaide?"

"Yeah, some . . . friends of mine."

"Go ahead! The more the merrier."

"Can I invite Buster?" asked Ben.

"And Marigold?" asked Samantha.

"Well, we can't very well have a picnic if we don't invite lots of hungry picnickers, can we?" Mrs. Haggerty stroked the puppy's back. "I want everyone to see my new pup. I think I'll name this critter Humphrey, after one of my favorite movie stars."

"Humphrey?"

"Don't you think it fits him?"

"Oh, yeah, Humphrey's a good name," said Kelly.

"Won't Arthur be surprised when he gets home! He's been wanting a good watchdog."

Mrs. Haggerty put Humphrey back into his box, where he immediately curled up for a nap. "Kelly, you run to Benchley's Market and fetch some hot dogs. I'll get the fire going. Ben, you run and cut some sticks from the woodpile."

"Uh, Mrs. Haggerty," said Ben. He put the receiver back on the telephone. "I just tried to call Buster. I think there's something wrong with your phone."

Mrs. Haggerty picked up the receiver and listened. "Fiddle-faddle. With all this wind, there must be a line down somewhere. A fine time. Better tell your parents."

"I'll go get Marigold," called Samantha. They all started for the front door.

"Just a minute." Mrs. Haggerty opened the hall closet and reached for her purse. "This should do it for the hot dogs. And here's a little extra for some candy canes."

"Thanks! We'll be right back."

"Hold on. Before you go running off like jackrabbits," she said, "I want to give you all a hug." They gathered about her, and she put her arms around the three of them, squeezing Ben in the middle. "You're the best friends an old lady like me ever had."

A little later, Kelly rang Jennifer's doorbell. She couldn't hide her happy face. She fairly bounced with excitement over the coming of Christmas, the new puppy, and the picnic. If only Jennifer and Adelaide would come. Kelly crossed her fingers and made a wish.

"Merry Christmas!" she shouted as Jennifer opened the door. Adelaide stood behind her, looking over her shoulder.

"Merry Christmas," said Jennifer.

"What are you doing?" asked Kelly.

"Nothing much," answered Jennifer.

"Actually, we're wrapping Christmas presents," said Adelaide. "It takes forever when you keep running out of tape."

"How'd you like to come over to Mrs. Haggerty's for a while?" Kelly asked. "Dad got her a puppy from Larry's farm. It's the cutest thing you ever saw! She's going to fix hot dogs for us, and we're going to toast marshmallows in the fireplace. Come on, OK?"

Jennifer looked at Adelaide. Adelaide shrugged her shoulders and pushed her glasses higher on her nose. "Gee, Kelly, we'd really like to, but we can't," Jennifer finally said.

"We've got a lot of stuff to wrap," said Adelaide.

"Don't you even want to see the new puppy?" The happy smile suddenly disappeared.

"We'll go over tomorrow. We've *got* to get this done," said Jennifer.

"You don't have to get anything done," said Kelly. "You just don't want to come."

"We can't," said Jennifer. "We have something important to do. It's a secret."

"You always have something important to do," said Kelly, "and you always have secrets. What's the matter with you two? Why don't you ever want to do anything with me anymore?" Her questions poured out. "I'm sorry

116

I almost broke your glasses, Adelaide. I really am. Can't you forget it?"

"Nothing's the matter," said Jennifer. "We've forgotten all about those Christmas cards."

"I still think you should have waited for me so we could have sold them together," said Kelly.

"I wish we had," replied Jennifer with a sigh.

"Next year we'll go together, OK?" said Adelaide.

"Next year I'm not ordering any," Kelly answered. "Come on, I want you to see the puppy. You'll love him. Mrs. Haggerty named him Humphrey."

"I don't know," said Jennifer.

"We'll go see the puppy tomorrow. We can't today," said Adelaide.

"I thought we could have a good time." Kelly turned to go and glanced back at her two friends. "I'll see you tomorrow . . . I guess." Intense disappointment welled up inside of her. She hoped it didn't show.

"Bye," said Jennifer.

"See you tomorrow," said Adelaide. She closed the door.

"Merry Christmas!" called Kelly. But nobody heard her. She felt an emptiness in the pit of her stomach as she trudged through the deep snow to Benchley's Market. She tried to hold back the terrible feeling of unhappiness that was growing inside her. Why didn't Jennifer and Adelaide want to be friends? What had she done?

She walked slower and slower. Suddenly she didn't even want to go to the party. What good was a party without her two best friends, anyway?

14

Marshmallows Toasting on an Open Fire

By the time Kelly returned to the house on Stewart Street, the picnic was in full swing. Mrs. Haggerty stirred the roaring fire in the fireplace while Ben and Buster held sticks with marshmallows over the flames. Samantha and Marigold sat at the edge of a large red-and-white checkered tablecloth spread on the floor. Humphrey ran around the parlor, sniffing the carpet and pouncing on dust balls in the corners.

"This is a great idea," said Ben. "A Christmas picnic, right here inside."

"When I was a young'un," said Mrs. Haggerty, "my brothers and I used to think the day before Christmas was the longest day of the year, so we always had a picnic on December 24. Mother fixed a picnic basket, and we pretended it was 102 degrees in the shade. We'd play blindman's buff and sing school songs and have a rollicking old time. We forgot all about the cold and the snow."

To think Mrs. Haggerty once had a mother and a father and brothers who all got together and played games and sang on Christmas Eve long ago. And now she was old. Kelly decided then and there that she would visit the Haggertys every day. Maybe she could get Jennifer and Adelaide to come, too. They could help around the house —take Humphrey for walks, wash windows, paint the fence, plant flowers, and listen to Mr. Haggerty's funny old farm stories.

"And when Tyler was a little tyke, we used to sing songs and toast marshmallows right here by this fireplace." Mrs. Haggerty chuckled. "Tyler always burned his marshmallows 'til they were crispy black. He said he liked them that way."

"Mrs. Haggerty, guess what I got you for Christmas." Kelly pulled a package from her pocket. It was wrapped in shiny red paper.

"You got me this rascal pup!"

"I got you something else, too. Here. Open it!"

Mrs. Haggerty sat down on the sofa. Humphrey immediately hopped into her lap and curled into a ball. She reached for the package and slowly pulled off the ribbon and the paper. Into her lap fell a cassette tape.

"Don't let Humphrey get it!" cried Kelly. "It's a tape I made of Robert Frost's poems. I read pages of them until the tape ran out. That gives you sixty whole minutes of poems that you can listen to whenever you want." Mrs. Haggerty held the tape and shook her head.

"Don't you like it?" asked Kelly.

"Like it? Why, I think this is wonderful! Humphrey and

I can sit by our fire here and listen to a poem any old time, can't we, Humphrey?" He lifted his head and thumped his tail on her knee.

"'Course, if you'd rather have *me* read to you, I'd be happy to."

"Thank you, Kelly." Mrs. Haggerty gave Kelly a hug.

"Where's your tape recorder? You said you had one, didn't you?" asked Kelly.

"It's over in that desk drawer. No, wait a minute. It's in the dining room—in the left side of the buffet."

Kelly opened four drawers of the buffet and finally found the tape recorder. "Want to hear a poem?"

"Oh, I'd like that very much."

"I got you this," piped up Samantha. She held up a crayon picture of a large Victorian house with icicles hanging from the eaves. "I made it last night."

Mrs. Haggerty took the picture and studied it carefully through her thick lenses. "This is a smart-looking picture. You even got the chimney with the smoke coming out. I'll hang it on the wall, right here."

Ben jumped up from his spot by the fire, walked to where his jacket hung in the hallway, and returned with a paper bag in his hand. "I got you something, too. Merry Christmas, Mrs. Haggerty."

"Ben, you sweet thing. What did you get an old lady like me?" Mrs. Haggerty reached in and pulled out another bag. "Doritos," she read, carefully pronouncing the word. She looked puzzled.

"They taste great," said Ben. "Here, let me show you." He opened the bag of Doritos and held it out. Mrs. Haggerty took a Dorito and bit into it.

"Mmm, good!" she said. "Thank you, Ben. Here, have some."

Ben dug in. "Thanks!"

Kelly pressed PLAY on the tape recorder, and soon the room was filled with her voice reading Robert Frost's poem, "Stopping by Woods on a Snowy Evening."

The doorbell rang. "I'll get it," she called as she jumped up and ran to the door. Jennifer and Adelaide stood on the porch, stomping their boots in the cold.

"Can we come in?" asked Jennifer.

"Sure!" Kelly wanted so much to be friends again, like they had always been. There was nothing worse than fighting with your best friends. "Come on in. I'll get you a hot dog." She reached for their jackets.

"Is this place really haunted?" whispered Adelaide. She stepped into the hallway and peered around the doorway into the library.

"There's just a ghost that lives in the parlor closet. That's all," whispered Kelly.

"You're joking, aren't you?" said Adelaide.

"Do I ever joke?"

"We got you a present," said Jennifer. She was unable to hide the gaily wrapped package behind her any longer.

"You did?"

"We've been working on this all week," added Adelaide. "We wanted to get it finished by today, but we didn't make it."

"Quiet, Adelaide. You'll give it away. Go on," said Jennifer, "open it."

Kelly looked at the package in her hands and back at Jennifer and Adelaide. "Hurry up, open it!" said Jennifer. "You're going to love it."

"Ok, I will, I will! But take your stuff off first, real quick. And come on in." Kelly waited until the girls had followed her into the parlor and greeted Mrs. Haggerty.

Mrs. Haggerty turned off the tape recorder. "You're Kelly's friends?"

"Yes," said Jennifer and Adelaide together. Kelly smiled.

"Weren't you that pretty princess who came to my door last Halloween?" Mrs. Haggerty asked Adelaide.

"Me?" Adelaide laughed her horsey laugh. "I wish! I was Gypsy Jezabubble, the famous witch."

"Come on, Kelly," coaxed Jennifer. "Open your present!"

Kelly ripped the paper from the box and pulled off the lid. "A rainbow!" She held up a latch-hook picture of a rainbow so that everyone could see. "Jennifer, it's beautiful. Thanks, Adelaide."

"That's what we were working on before, when you came," explained Adelaide.

"Trying to get it done," said Jennifer. "Gosh, there was more work to that than we ever thought!"

"It's supposed to be a pillow, but we'll have to finish it some other time. We decided to come over here today." Adelaide patted the puppy on Mrs. Haggerty's lap.

"Do you have any idea how long that took us?" exclaimed Jennifer. She held up her hands. "My fingers are in great pain!"

"I have something for you, too," said Kelly. "I'll be back in a split second. Don't go!"

Kelly threw on her hat and jacket, ran home, and brought back the presents for Jennifer and Adelaide. The looks on their faces as they opened them convinced her that friends were always friends. They might have an argument or two now and then, but a friend would always come back.

122

Jennifer fastened her pin to her sweater. "You know I love unicorns, don't you?" she said as she threw her arm around Kelly's shoulder.

"I wanted to get you a real live one, but I couldn't find one." Kelly laughed.

"You didn't need to get me anything," said Jennifer.

"I wanted to."

Adelaide opened her present and grinned when she held up the tiny hot-air balloon. It swung gently from her fingers. "I'll hang it in my room. It's terrific, Kelly. Thanks!"

"A picnic is no picnic without a game of croquet," announced Mrs. Haggerty. She pulled an old croquet set from the hall closet and rolled it into the parlor.

"Croquet!" Samantha and Marigold clapped their hands.

"Here? Inside?" asked Buster.

"Why not?" said Mrs. Haggerty. "Instead of wickets, though, we'll need some colored paper circles. When you hit your ball, it has to cross over a paper circle before it can go on to the next one. The first person to cross the red circle wins. Tyler used to play this with all his friends."

Mrs. Haggerty showed everyone how to cut out the paper circles, number them from one to ten, and place them on the floor. Before long the eight of them were chatting and laughing as they whacked the old wooden croquet balls around the parlor floor. The grandfather clock struck three. The fire in the fireplace crackled softly.

After the croquet game, Mrs. Haggerty brought a cooler from the kitchen filled with ice and Cokes. They all gathered around the fireplace and roasted more hot dogs and marshmallows. Kelly filled her paper plate with baked beans and potato chips and stretched out on the floor beside Adelaide and Jennifer.

"Care to see my picture?" Mrs. Haggerty passed her picture around for everyone to see. "Isn't that a sight! An old lady like me pounding on the piano. Kelly and Ben recorded my song, too. I sent it to Tyler last week."

"What song?" asked Adelaide.

"Mrs. Haggerty wrote her very own song. You should hear it!" said Kelly.

"I'd like to," said Adelaide.

"Can you really sing?" asked Buster. He took the last bite of his hot dog.

"Sure I can sing," answered Mrs. Haggerty. "I might sound like an old goose, but I can sing."

They moved to the library. While Mrs. Haggerty played the piano and sang her song, Kelly leaned over and whispered into Ben's ear. He looked up, surprised, and then he grinned. He leaned over and whispered into Buster's ear. Buster smiled and winked at Ben. Ben winked at Kelly. Kelly pulled the ripped picture from her pocket, held the two pieces together, and showed it to Jennifer.

"That's the ghost," she whispered. "See that? That white shadow in the closet."

"It is?"

"What else could it be?" answered Kelly. Ben and Buster nodded their heads up and down and squeezed their lips together, trying not to smile.

Adelaide and Jennifer glanced about the room nervously. "There's a ghost in this room right now? This minute?" Jennifer asked.

"Shhh!" Kelly raised her finger to her lips. "Don't say anything."

124

"But . . . a ghost?"

"Don't worry. It's not in this room."

"Where is it?" demanded Jennifer. Her eyes were about to pop out.

"In the closet in the parlor." Jennifer and Adelaide twisted around and looked through the hallway into the parlor.

"You haven't seen anything!" whispered Ben, joining in. "You ought to go inside the secret stairway up to the attic. You can hear it in there."

"That's right," said Kelly. "Samantha and me—we were trapped inside that stairway, and we heard this horrible breathing right down our necks and big, heavy footsteps!"

"That was Buster," said Samantha, joining the conversation.

"Samantha!" Kelly covered Samantha's mouth.

"There's no ghost in here," said Adelaide. She pushed the picture away.

"Yeah, you're just tricking us," added Jennifer.

"If you say so." Kelly shrugged her shoulders and shoved the torn picture back into her pocket.

After a few more minutes, Mrs. Haggerty ended her song and stood up. "What do you think?" she asked.

Everyone clapped their hands. Buster whistled. "It's a wonderful song," said Jennifer. She stood up and started for the hall. "Thanks a lot for the party, Mrs. Haggerty. I have to go now, though. It's getting late."

"Well now, girls, you can't possibly run off yet. You just got here."

"I'll help you clean up," said Kelly.

"We'll all help," they said.

"Wanna see the secret stairway?" Ben asked Adelaide. "It's really something. Come on, I'll show you."

"No, I don't think so," said Adelaide.

Jennifer hurried to the parlor and began picking up empty Coke bottles and paper plates. As she passed the parlor closet, she heard a strange scratching sound at the door. She stopped and listened. The scratching continued. "Hey, Kelly! Adelaide! Come here. I hear something." She reached for the doorknob and turned it. And then she screamed.

15

The Creature in the Closet

A gray mouse darted out and ran between her feet. Coke cans and paper plates flew into the air. Jennifer screamed again. "A mouse! Catch it!" Everyone rushed into the parlor to see what all the commotion was about.

"Wow! What a mess you made," said Buster.

"There's a mouse in here! Did you see it?" Her words tumbled out, one on top of the other. "It was big! Maybe a rat! I think it went under the sofa. Yes, I'm sure that's where it is. I almost died!" Jennifer grew increasingly dramatic now that her scare had ended.

"This is great!" said Ben. "Just what I wanted—a hamster. Get back, I'll get him." He dropped to his knees and peeked under the sofa.

"That was no hamster," said Jennifer. "It was a rat! Huge! With sharp fangs. It almost killed me. Be careful, Ben."

"Don't stick your nose under there like that," warned Kelly. "What if it bites?"

"I hate mice," said Marigold. "I wanna go home."

"Look out, Ben," screamed Samantha. "It's gonna get away!" She scrambled to the far corner of the room.

"Just a minute. I'll go get my mousetrap," said Mrs. Haggerty.

"GOT HIM!" yelled Ben. He hopped to his feet.

Samantha screamed.

"No problem at all," said Ben. He gripped the top of the Doritos bag. "He's right in here. And he's all mine. I caught him."

"You can have him," said Adelaide.

"He's going to gnaw straight through that bag any second," warned Buster.

"You're right. Can I have the box we brought Humphrey in, Mrs. Haggerty?"

"Why, sure. Take it. And take the mouse, too," she said.

"Thanks!" said Ben. He put on his jacket and picked up the box, with the Doritos bag and the mouse inside. "This is going to be a great Christmas!"

"Better tell Mom you're bringing that mouse in the house," said Kelly.

"No way! I'm gonna surprise her tomorrow. Come on, Samantha." Samantha, Marigold, and Buster followed Ben out the front door. "Merry Christmas, Mrs. Haggerty!" they called.

"Merry Christmas!" she answered.

Jennifer, Adelaide, and Kelly stayed behind to help straighten the house. They picked up the Coke cans and paper plates, washed a few dishes, carried out the garbage, and finally took Humphrey outside, where he scampered in the snow, sniffed, and finally did what he was supposed to do. "Good boy," said Kelly. "Good dog." They brought him back inside.

"We'll be back tomorrow," Kelly said. "Mom's bringing some fudge. Are you sure you don't want to come over to our house for a little while tonight?"

"No, Kelly. I think I'll just sit here by my fire and write a letter to Tyler. I'll be sure to put this good-lookin' picture of me along with it," she answered with a sad smile. Mrs. Haggerty sat next to the fireplace, her hands folded neatly in her lap.

"Merry Christmas, Mrs. Haggerty," said Kelly. She hugged the old woman.

"Merry Christmas, Kelly." She started to get up, but Kelly told her to stay in her comfortable chair. They would see themselves to the door.

'Twas the night before Christmas,
  when all through the house
Not a creature was stirring,
  not even a mouse. . . .

chanted Kelly as she reached for her jacket. "The mouse is stirring at *my* house now, thanks to Ben."

"A Christmas mouse," said Mrs. Haggerty. Humphrey jumped into her lap and licked her hands. She stroked his velvet ears.

"If you have any more mice, just call Ben. He's better than any mousetrap," said Kelly.

The doorbell rang. Humphrey growled. "Now who could that be?" asked Mrs. Haggerty.

Kelly opened the door and was startled to see a man

dressed in an overcoat and hat standing on the porch. A large suitcase stood by his feet. He gripped a smaller satchel in his hand. "Hi!" he said, equally surprised to see Kelly.

"Just a minute," said Kelly. She shot into the parlor. "Mrs. Haggerty, there's some guy at the door for you. Look out, I think he's a salesman—probably selling vacuum cleaners or something. This is a funny time to be—" But before Kelly could finish, the man entered the house, crossed the hall, and stood directly behind her.

"Not selling a thing today!" He laughed.

"Tyler!" Mrs. Haggerty smiled her broadest smile and reached toward her son. Humphrey leaped from her lap and circled Tyler, yipping and wagging his tail. Tyler dropped both suitcases to the floor. He walked to his mother and wrapped his arms around her, giving her a long hug and kissing her cheek.

Kelly glanced at Adelaide and Jennifer. "Let's go," she whispered. They nodded in agreement and began to back toward the door.

"Tyler, Tyler, how good it is to see you!" exclaimed Mrs. Haggerty. "And right here on Christmas Eve. What a surprise!" Her face radiated happiness. Humphrey had stopped his yapping and was busy sniffing at Tyler's shoes.

"I'll tell you, Mom, it feels great to be home." He hugged her one more time and then took off his hat and coat and began to warm his hands by the fire.

"Don't go, girls, for heaven's sake, I want you to meet my boy." She motioned for them to come back. "Tyler, this is Kelly, Jennifer, and Adelaide from over on Hopper Street. Kelly brought me this little critter for Christmas." She pointed to the puppy.

Greetings were exchanged all around. Finally, Tyler got down on his hands and knees and shook Humphrey's paw. Humphrey playfully chewed on Tyler's hand.

"I told you I'd be home for Christmas, and it looks like I just made it."

"You did?" Mrs. Haggerty was puzzled. "You never told me any such thing."

"I wrote a letter, but I guess I beat it here. And yesterday I tried to call, but I never could get through."

"My telephone's not working."

"It was a last-minute break. We finished filming two weeks earlier than we thought, so I decided to fly back. I'll tell you, with this weather, most of the flights were canceled."

"Oh, Tyler, you just don't know how tickled I am to see you," said Mrs. Haggerty. "What a wonderful Christmas this is."

"I just had to come home, Mom," said Tyler. "I had to tell you how much I liked your song." He pulled the tape from his pocket.

"Oh, Tyler, did you really like it?"

"I loved it." Tyler hugged her.

Mrs. Haggerty leaned her head against Tyler's shoulder. "I'm so glad you're home."

"I am, too. And tomorrow we're going to the hospital."

"We're going to see Arthur?" Mrs. Haggerty was almost too overjoyed to speak. "It will be so nice, so nice. All of us together again. Lordy, it's been such an awful long time."

"I know, Mom. Too long." He grinned. "Doctor Gallitin says Dad is feeling much better. He says a few more days and the medicine should be regulated just right."

"That's good." Mrs. Haggerty stood up. "Come in here, Tyler. We have a surprise for you, don't we, girls?" She winked at Kelly, Jennifer, and Adelaide. They followed Mrs. Haggerty across the hall and into the library.

"Wait!" called Kelly. She slid to the floor and plugged the cord into the wall socket. The Christmas tree suddenly shone with lights of red, blue, green, and yellow, turning the dreary library into a room of bright enchantment. The tinsel star twinkled at the top.

"It's beautiful," said Tyler. He put his arm around his mother's waist. "And there's my wooden soldier!"

"Right on the front—just where it always goes."

"I made the cranberry and popcorn chain," said Kelly.

"Looks good," said Tyler. "Can I eat it?"

Kelly laughed. "My sister helped. You'll get to meet her tomorrow. Oh, wait. You're going to the hospital tomorrow. I almost forgot."

"Not until the afternoon," said Tyler.

"Now your mama promised," said Mrs. Haggerty. "You're all coming tomorrow morning for eggnog. You, too, girls," she said to Jennifer and Adelaide. "We'll have a nice Christmas visit."

Kelly picked up the puppy. "Are you taking Humphrey with you to the hospital?"

Mrs. Haggerty thought a moment. "I don't believe those hospitals allow critters. Especially frisky little pups like this one." She patted Humphrey's head. "How about taking Humphrey home with you tomorrow and dog-sitting for a few days? Would you do that for me?"

"Sure, Mrs. Haggerty! I wouldn't mind that a bit!"

It was almost twilight as the three girls hurried down Stewart Street. They looked at all the Christmas trees in the windows. Most of them were already aglow with lights. "Isn't that great? Mrs. Haggerty is going to get to see her husband on Christmas, after all," said Kelly. "I'll never forget how sad she looked just before Tyler showed up. Remember?"

"Yeah, she did," agreed Jennifer.

"We ought to visit her a lot," suggested Adelaide.

"Not if there's mice in her house," said Jennifer.

Kelly laughed. "We can set out some mousetraps and cheese. I wouldn't want Humphrey to get bitten on the nose by a mouse."

"Or we could set Ben loose." They all laughed. It felt so good to be with Jennifer and Adelaide again. She liked making a new friend like Mrs. Haggerty. New friends were exciting, full of different ideas. But old friends were great, too. They knew each other, inside and out.

Kelly clutched her present in her left arm and threw her right arm across Jennifer's shoulder. "Boy, was I glad to see you at the party today."

"It's no fun fighting," said Jennifer. "No more, OK?"

"And no more secrets, unless you include me in," said Kelly. She thought about the secret latch-hook pillow project. "Promise?"

"Promise. Secrets are impossible to keep," said Adelaide. "It's easier to keep . . . a ghost in a closet!" They laughed and broke into a run, cutting through the backyards and hopping over the stones in the frozen creek.